COLLECTOR'S GUIDE

written by
Maggie Fischer

studio fun
INTERNATIONAL

studio fun INTERNATIONAL

Studio Fun International
An imprint of Printers Row Publishing Group
A division of Readerlink Distribution Services, LLC
10350 Barnes Canyon Road, Suite 100, San Diego, CA 92121
www.studiofun.com

Written by Maggie Fischer
Illustrated by Hasbro
Designed by Jenna Riggs

Library of Congress Cataloging-in-Publication Data is available upon request.

Printers Row Publishing Group is a division of Readerlink Distribution Services, LLC. Studio Fun International is a registered trademark of Readerlink Distribution Services, LLC. All notations of errors or omissions should be addressed to Studio Fun International, Editorial Department, at the above address.

ISBN: 978-0-7944-4386-3

Manufactured, printed, and assembled in Shenzhen, China.

First printing, January 2019. RRD/01/19

23 22 21 20 19 1 2 3 4 5

Contents

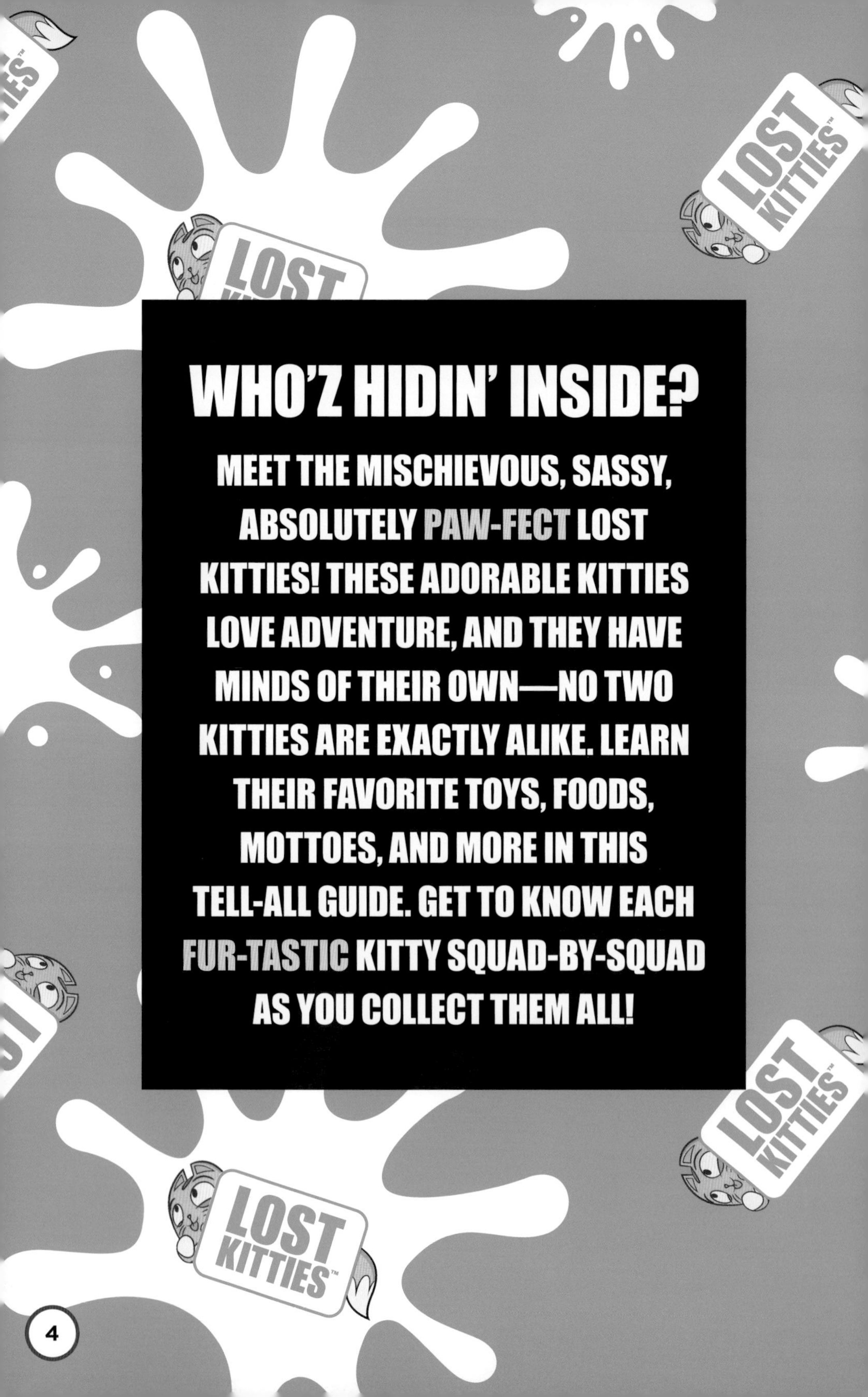

WHO'Z HIDIN' INSIDE?

MEET THE MISCHIEVOUS, SASSY, ABSOLUTELY PAW-FECT LOST KITTIES! THESE ADORABLE KITTIES LOVE ADVENTURE, AND THEY HAVE MINDS OF THEIR OWN—NO TWO KITTIES ARE EXACTLY ALIKE. LEARN THEIR FAVORITE TOYS, FOODS, MOTTOES, AND MORE IN THIS TELL-ALL GUIDE. GET TO KNOW EACH FUR-TASTIC KITTY SQUAD-BY-SQUAD AS YOU COLLECT THEM ALL!

SINGLE
KITTIES

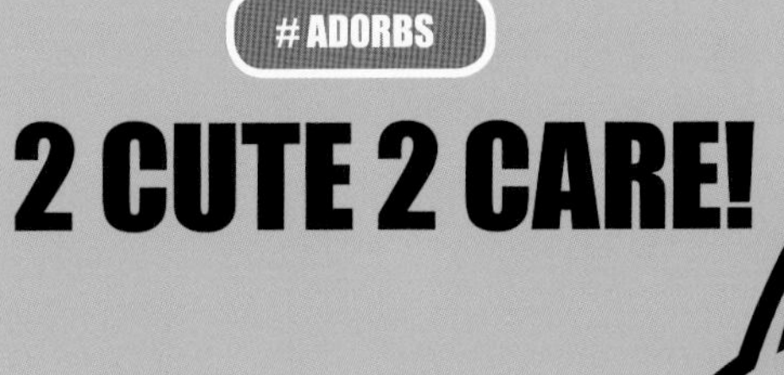

2 CUTE 2 CARE!

MEET
Memez!

ADORBS

SERIES 1

What's that? So cute you're speechless? Memez gets that a lot. When he's **FELINE GOOD**, you'll catch him sticking out his teeny tiny tongue—blep! This too-cute kitty is always **MILKIN' IT** for the crowd, and when he sings, every kitty puts their paws in the air like they just don't care! Sometimes he needs a hug for luck before he takes the stage, but Memez loves a sparkling spotlight, so he just has to keep reminding himself **PURRS BEFORE NERVES**!

LIKES: Being the center of attention
DISLIKES: Being the center of attention
FAVORITE SNACK: Beans and mice
HOBBIES: Singing, dancing, FURRISBEE golf
FAVORITE TOY: Catnip banana
MOTTO: "Free hugz!"
LIFE DREAM: To perform on every stage in the world!

MEET
Pixie Purrs!

#ADORBS

SERIES 1

Pixie Purrs's favorite cat bed is whatever laptop you're currently using. But nobody dares touch her once she's settled in for a catnap, because she's just too cute to move! This zen kitty can contort into all kinds of shapes, and her flexibility comes in handy when tucking herself into tiny napping spots. Pixie Purrs uses yoga to cleanse her PAW-KRAS—her favorite pose is Downward-Facing Cat. Nothing ruffles Pixie Purrs's fur, and she often pops up where you least expect her, already in a full snooze!

LIKES: Heating pads, laptop keyboards
DISLIKES: Loud noises, negative energy
FAVORITE SNACK: Pineapple pizza
HOBBIES: Yoga, MEOWDITATION
FAVORITE TOY: Red ball of yarn
MOTTO: "May the feline in meh purr to the feline in u. Namas-tail."
LIFE DREAM: To do yoga at the PAWJ MAHAL.

MEET
Tickles!

#ADORBS

SERIES 1

The world is a FUR-LARIOUS place for ticklish Tickles. This silly kitty loves to laugh, but he's always on the lookout for floating feathers and poking paws, because once he gets going, he can't seem to stop! Sometimes he has a little trouble pronouncing his "L's" and "R's" but somehow his speech IMPURRDIMENT only makes this kitty cuter! Tickles can turn any day around with his giggly meow, and his PAWSITIVE attitude makes him a great FURRIEND!

LIKES: Jokes, pranks, butterflies
DISLIKES: Tickle fights, PAW-DICURES
FAVORITE SNACK: Snickerdoodles
HOBBIES: Stand-up PAWMEDY, air hockey
FAVORITE TOY: Cuddles, his stuffed animal starfish
MOTTO: "Wyfe is bettah when yoh waffing (Life is better when you're laughing)!"
LIFE DREAM: To open a butterfly sanctuary

MEET
Bonbon!

\# ADORBS

SERIES 1

Bonbon loves everykitty. No, really. When she's not writing love letters to all ninety of her best **FURRIENDS**, she's baking sugary treats to share! Bonbon's sweet just like her favorite **MARSHMEOW** candies, and even though she's got fabulous green fur, she's never green with envy. Bonbon loves to bake, but she's pretty **FUR-GETFUL,** so she always makes more than she meant to. Oh, well! That just means there's more to share with all of the friends she hasn't met yet!

LIKES: Everyone, everything
DISLIKES: Running out of flour
FAVORITE SNACK: MARSHMEOW candy
HOBBIES: Baking, hugging, smiling
FAVORITE TOY: Purple oven timer
MOTTO: "There's alwayz room in the recipe 4 more friends!"
LIFE DREAM: To bake the world's biggest cookie

MEET
Nap-kin!

\# ADORBS

SERIES 1

Nap-kin is a world-famous kitty physicist with a **MEOWSTER'S DEGREE** in Aerospace Engineering. But a brain that big needs a lot of power, so he can usually be found in a deep snooze in the nearest patch of sunlight. He seems like he's snoring, but rest assured, this feline genius is planning his next big move to the final **FUR-RONTIER**. His eyes are usually closed, but his paws are always twitching, because this little kitty has big dreams!

LIKES: Warm milk, books about space
DISLIKES: Alarm clocks
FAVORITE SNACK: Pigs in a blanket
HOBBIES: Napping, stargazing
FAVORITE TOY: Laser light
MOTTO: "That's one small snoozle for Nap-kin, one giant snoozle for kittykind!"
LIFE DREAM: To be the first CAT-STRONAUT to land on Mars!

MEET
Gato!

Gato never sits still for long. Always tapping his paws and looking out windows, Gato's better when he's roaming. This kitty is up for anything, and his **PURR-O-METER** is permanently set to "stoked!" Sneaking milk from a local farm while the cows remain clueless? He's so there. Dumpster diving for any extra fishy bits that some kitty might have been foolish enough to throw away? Duh, let's do this! Catnip gardening? Do you even have to ask?

LIKES: Adventure
DISLIKES: Negative attitudes
FAVORITE SNACK: Catnip cream cheese
HOBBIES: Road-tripping, surfing, making FURRIENDS
FAVORITE TOY: A mini Gato made of fabric
MOTTO: "Success!"
LIFE DREAM: To give a little love back to the world before his nine lives are up

MEET
Gertrude!

Gertrude has the daintiest twinkle paws and the **ATTI-TUTU-TUDE** to back them up. This ballerina is like catnip onstage, and when she's twirling in mid-pirouette, no kitty can look away! But even though she may seem sweet when she dazzles with her **PAW DE BOURRÉS**, her eyes are always sharply on the audience. She has a strict no-photos-allowed **PAWLICY**, and once gracefully launched herself off of the stage and tackled a kitty in the audience who tried to snap a selfie in the middle of a show. This **PURR-ANCING QUEEN** means business!

LIKES: Brand-new tutus, PAW-FORMING
DISLIKES: Fan photos, PAW-PARAZZI
FAVORITE SNACK: Gummy mice
HOBBIES: Choreographing routines, sewing CAT-STUMES
FAVORITE TOY: Her pointe shoes, specially made for her paws
MOTTO: "On Tutu Tuezdayz, we wear pink!"
LIFE DREAM: To dance the lead in Swan Lake

MEET
Boo-ger!

#ADORBS  SERIES 2

A growl pierces the night air. The cold night settles in and the growling becomes louder as the leaves of a nearby bush start to rustle. A hole in the bush sloooowly opens up—BOO! Oh, whew. It's only Boo-ger. His tummy is growling. See, Boo-ger the bat cat is not very spooky, but don't tell him that. This FUR-OCIOUS kitty comes alive on YOWL-A-WEEN and PAW-TIES all year long until the next October. The other kitties humor him when he bares his little fangs, but no one is really scared of him. Although, he does tend to catnap upside-down...

LIKES:	Ghosts, goblins, monsters
DISLIKES:	Not being taken seriously, garlic
FAVORITE SNACK:	O-negative catnip
HOBBIES:	Haunting, stalking, bobbing for apples
FAVORITE TOY:	Tissue paper ghost
MOTTO:	"I vant to drink some milkz!"
LIFE DREAM:	To go down in HISS-TORY as the most FANG-TASTIC bat cat there ever was

MEET
Baller!

#ADORBS  SERIES 2

If you're trying to find roly-poly Baller, all you have to do is look down. Farther. A liiiiitle farther—ah, there she is! This too-cute kitty is always ready to play, and yarn is her FUR-VORITE way to get her paws moving. But even though Baller is the daughter of a PURR-LEM GLOBETROTTER and a PAW-FESSIONAL YARNBALL CATHLETE, she's not playing for points. She bats yarn balls for the love of the game, hugging her favorite yarn tight as she rolls away the day. But sometimes she gets stuck on the carpet and needs someone to lend a paw. Help a kitty out!

LIKES:	Angora wool, cashmere
DISLIKES:	Knots
FAVORITE SNACK:	Candy covered in floor fuzz
HOBBIES:	Yarnball, somersaulting
FAVORITE TOY:	Yellow ball of yarn
MOTTO:	"Stop, drop, and ROLL!"
LIFE DREAM:	To coach a LICKLE LEAGUE Yarnball team

#CATHLETIC

WORK OUT THOSE WHISKERZ

MEET

Mr. Mush!

#CATHLETIC

SERIES 1

Spilled milk has met its match in Mr. Mush! A retired sumo kitty from the heart of Japan, Mr. Mush is always up for a challenge. Although he doesn't say much, a good knock-knock joke never fails to have his whiskers twitching into a smile! Calm in a crisis and taller than most kitties combined, his purple paws are steady and his game face is ready. When it's **MEOW OR NEVER**, the rest of the kitties know Mr. Mush will **STEP UP TO THE TUNA PLATE**!

LIKES: Sushi, knock-knock jokes
DISLIKES: Tight spaces
FAVORITE SNACK: A CALI-FUR-NIA ROLL
HOBBIES: Sumo wrestling, eating PAWPSICLES
FAVORITE TOY: Glow-in-the-dark fish
MOTTO: "The perfect time to start is right meow!"
LIFE DREAM: To teach sumo wrestling to aspiring kittens

MEET

Thimble!

\# CATHLETIC

SERIES 1

It might look like he's tangled up in yarn, but Thimble has a plan. Thimble always has a plan. Big eyes and yellow fur make this teeny kitty seem innocent, but he's usually **UP TO SOMETHING**. This flexible feline melts around obstacles like liquid—he's been named the limbo champion in over 100 competitions. The other kitties aren't sure what he's training for when he spends all that time zigzagging through yarn, but whatever it is: he's more than ready.

LIKES: Spy movies, knitting supplies
DISLIKES: Surprises
FAVORITE SNACK: Red licorice ropes
HOBBIES: Stealing knitting, getting caught with stolen knitting, running off with stolen knitting
FAVORITE TOY: Multicolored yarn
MOTTO: "Pay no attention to the kitteh behind the yarn."
LIFE DREAM: To pull off the greatest heist in kitty knitting history

MEET

Pepp!

\# CATHLETIC

SERIES 1

The fur is always flying when Pepp is on the scene! The youngest of a litter of twelve, Pepp is the Energizer Kitty. Impulse control isn't really her thing—she wants what she wants and she wants it **RIGHT MEOW**, thank you very much! If you're looking for Pepp, you can find her as high up as her tail will take her: the tallest tree branch, the corner cabinet in the kitchen, or flying right at you, paws outstretched!

LIKES: Heights
DISLIKES: Waiting
FAVORITE SNACK: Instant Mac and Cheese
HOBBIES: Climbing, Leaping, Falling
FAVORITE TOY: Bright orange feather
MOTTO: "Iz a bird, iz a plane, iz PEPP!"
LIFE DREAM: To climb the tallest mountain in the world

MEET

Sketch!

SERIES 1

Now you see her—now you don't! Sketch is the fastest kitty on four paws, and she's always got her whiskers in some milk. No matter where you hide the milk cartons, she'll find them, and they're usually gone before you can blink. This stealthy feline is a one-cat operation; she doesn't need ANYKITTY to hang out with, and no, that's certainly not the bright blue flash of her fur that you see following you from room-to-room, watching...waiting...

LIKES: Milk, chocolate milk, strawberry milk
DISLIKES: Locked refrigerators
FAVORITE SNACK: Sprinkle swirl milkshake
HOBBIES: Pickpocketing, fridge-raiding
FAVORITE TOY: Lime green fish
MOTTO: "Go ahead. Milk my day."
LIFE DREAM: To sail across a sea of milk like a dairy ferry

MEET

Scoops!

CATHLETIC

SERIES 1

Scoops is as chill as they come, but the cone of shame is really cramping his style. This **SKATERCAT** has mad skills, and when he's not doing ollies and **KITTYFLIPS** on the half-pipe, he's cruising through the kitchen to crush some organic unsweetened almond milk. Get him talking and you'll find that he has a story for every bruise on his tail, and even though he owns more bandages than every other kitty combined, he won't slow down unless his board breaks!

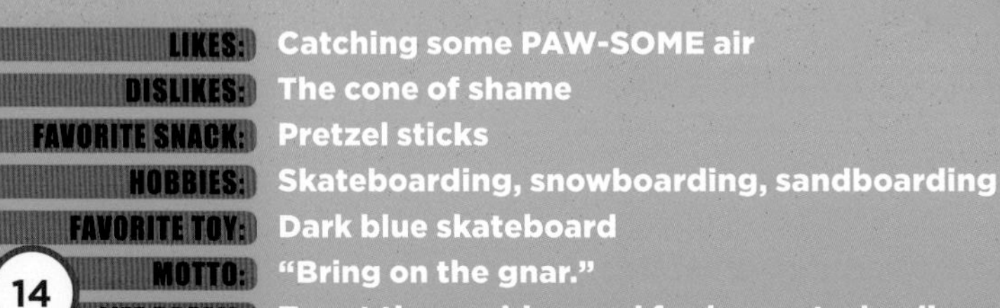
LIKES: Catching some PAW-SOME air
DISLIKES: The cone of shame
FAVORITE SNACK: Pretzel sticks
HOBBIES: Skateboarding, snowboarding, sandboarding
FAVORITE TOY: Dark blue skateboard
MOTTO: "Bring on the gnar."
LIFE DREAM: To set the world record for longest wheelie

MEET
Wheelz!

SERIES 2

Wheelz used to be the best bicyclist on four paws, but four years ago he had a mishap at the TOUR DE FURRANCE. He entered as a FUR-OCIOUS competitor, but after a couple of miles, a yellow jacket flew right at his whiskers, and Wheelz tumbled to the ground! Ever since, he's been too scaredy-cat to get on another bike. To PAW-PARE for his big comeback, Wheelz practices on an invisible bicycle, which he claims has all of the same benefits. Wheelz will get his little heart pedaling again; he just needs a little more time on the invisible trails.

LIKES: Bug spray, helmets
DISLIKES: Falling
FAVORITE SNACK: Peppermint candies
HOBBIES: Invisible cycling, invisible trail riding, invisible weight training
FAVORITE TOY: Purple bicycle bell
MOTTO: "Just keep cycling!"
LIFE DREAM: To win the TOUR DE FURRANCE

MEET
Boops!

CATHLETIC

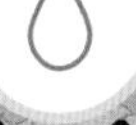

SERIES 2

Boops has been working so hard that she's gotten used to sleeping in the handstand PAW-SITION—training never stops for this FUR-RIFFIC gymnast kitty! Boops has been famous for her PURRFECT back handspring ever since she was a kitten, and so she twists and twirls on a daily basis to uphold her sterling REPAWTATION. Sure, sometimes her tail gets caught underneath the balance beam, and she shaved off a bit of her whiskers when she came too close to the vault, but don't let her asymmetrical fur fool you: she's ready to boop to the top.

LIKES: The feeling of chalk on her paws
DISLIKES: Hitting the mat
FAVORITE SNACK: Licorice ropes
HOBBIES: Planking, doing triple cat-wheels
FAVORITE TOY: Her special sparkly leotard
MOTTO: "Stick it to dah mat!"
LIFE DREAM: To take home the gold at the PAW-LYMPICS

MEET Maxwell!

Maxwell is a gamer extraordinaire. His setup includes five monitors on and above his massive desk. Maxwell can play CALL OF MEW-TY with a team of eighteen spread across different continents while tinkering with his WORLD OF WHISKERCRAFT characters AND earning the high score in FURT-NITE. But despite his MEOWSTER multitasking skills, Maxwell has *no* chill. His fur is as red as his temper, and can be heard yowling about "N00bz" from four blocks away.

LIKES: High scores, power-ups
DISLIKES: Slow Wi-Fi
FAVORITE SNACK: Blue-flavored MOUNTAIN MEW
HOBBIES: Defeating other kitties online
FAVORITE TOY: His retro white mouse controller
MOTTO: "Why get a life when I already haz nine?"
LIFE DREAM: To become the greatest gamer ever known

MEET Flipz!

CATHLETIC
SERIES 2

Are you watching? Are you **FUR SURE** watching? Because you do NOT want to miss this. Topsy-turvy Flipz loves showing off for her fellow kitties; she can do forty backflips in a row—on a bad day. Flipz uses her upside-down antics to her full advantage. Crouching on top of the kitchen cabinets, she'll wait for a kitty to put some milk in the fridge, and...FLIP! She'll spring from her hiding place in a perfect dive, circling once, twice, SCORE! Nabbing the milk in cotton candy-colored paws, she's backflipping out the door before kitties can say, "Mew?"

LIKES: Attention, feeling dizzy
DISLIKES: Keeping her paws on the ground
FAVORITE SNACK: Coconut milk all frothy from flipping
HOBBIES: Diving, daring, dazzling
FAVORITE TOY: Her slinky
MOTTO: "The upside-down's not so bad."
LIFE DREAM: To win a televised talent show with her PAW-SOME flipping routine

MEET Ohai!

SERIES 1

Sleepy little Ohai's head tilt has a hypnotic quality. When she blinks up at you with those big eyes, it's hard to remember what you were doing before. Ohai claims she went to school for a FUR-LOSOPHY degree, but she owns a CLAWFUL LOT of books about witchcraft for someone who says her favorite author is PAWCRETES. Ohai has a way of convincing even the surliest kitties to give her what she wants, whether that's a hug, some milk, or their car.

LIKES: Crystals, candles
DISLIKES: Questions
FAVORITE SNACK: Pixie sticks
HOBBIES: Mysteriously chanting, reading
FAVORITE TOY: Teeny yellow bird
MOTTO: "Oh...HI!"
LIFE DREAM: To visit Salem, CAT-SACHUSSETS

MEET Pants!

SERIES 1

Prankster Pants is always itching for some mischief, so be on the lookout in case he gets his paws on whoopee cushions or some super glue! Clever Pants is constantly coming up with new ways to tease his FURRIENDS. Kitties caught in Pants's path come out the other side with paws covered in peanut butter, marker mustaches on their whiskers, and tails tied into twists! Pants is sneaky, but so silly that his trademark chuckle usually gets him caught!

LIKES: Pranks, jokes
DISLIKES: Rules
FAVORITE SNACK: Boston cream pie
HOBBIES: Replacing milk with mayonnaise, covering scratching posts in sticky tape
FAVORITE TOY: Blue banana peel
MOTTO: "When u haz no pants, u haz no pants to lose."
LIFE DREAM: To pants the president

MEET

Chickie!

Chickie has been there, seen that. With all the latest from PETFLIX, MEWLU, and H-FLEA-O GO right at his PAWTIPS, he is always on top of kitty culture. Sure, he spends most of his time inside, but his couch is his castle, and he is the undisputed ruler of the kingdom. Chickie may seem bored as he flips through channel after channel, but he knows television like the tip of his tail, and he'll always pick the perfect show that EVERYKITTY wants to watch.

LIKES: SCI-FUR Thrillers
DISLIKES: Reruns
FAVORITE SNACK: Movie theater buttered popcorn
HOBBIES: Channel surfing, watching movie marathons
FAVORITE TOY: The remote
MOTTO: "YAS, I'm still watching."
LIFE DREAM: To create his own movie streaming service

MEET

Tummy Tum!

\# CATTITUDE
SERIES 1

Tummy Tum has the tiniest tummy, but it's very hard to fill. Sure, there was that one Thanksgiving that she had a fresh minnow inside of a salmon fillet inside of a marinated tuna stuffed into a deep-fried swordfish flambéed on a bed of chicken nuggets...but that was just the appetizer course! Tummy Tum has a deep appreciation for food, and really savors the .0003 seconds it takes to dip a monster-sized turkey leg down her throat. BON APPÉTIT!

LIKES: Breakfast, lunch, dinner, snacks, tea
DISLIKES: An empty refrigerator
FAVORITE SNACK: The pantry
HOBBIES: Eating, dreaming about eating, jazzercise
FAVORITE TOY: Fuzzy pink turkey leg
MOTTO: "If at first u don't swallow, chew, chew, chew again!"
LIFE DREAM: To eat an entire restaurant's food in one sitting

MEET

Flush!

IFIFITS

SERIES 1

Life is in the toilet for furry Flush, and that's exactly how she likes it! In her eyes, nothing beats **SPLISH-SPLASHING** in a safe and cozy bowl, especially when you cannonballed your way in there to begin with! Cute as a button and nearly too small to spot, Flush can go missing for weeks at a time. But be careful where you sit, because she always turns up eventually—usually in the bathroom you were just about to use!

LIKES:	**Toilet bowls, bidets, sinks**
DISLIKES:	**The hot, itchy feeling of dry fur**
FAVORITE SNACK:	**Soap**
HOBBIES:	**Swimming, diving, hiding**
FAVORITE TOY:	**Rubber duck**
MOTTO:	**"Life's a bowl! CANNONBALL!"**
LIFE DREAM:	**To swan dive into a solid gold toilet bowl**

MEET

J. Roly!

IFIFITS

SERIES 1

Yes, he knows there is a jar on his head. He fit it in there all by himself. Are you impressed? Rumor has it that J. Roly was born in an alley between a recording studio and a hip-hop club. He's got a beat in his feet and the flail in his tail, and no one can stop his **DYNA-BITE** dancing! When he's not hitting the bongo jars, he's laying down some sweet break-dancing moves. Turn up the funk and watch J. Roly two-step and slide into his signature move: spinning on his head!

LIKES:	**Tuna cans, pickle jars**
DISLIKES:	**Sitting still**
FAVORITE SNACK:	**Jelly**
HOBBIES:	**Drumming, break-dancing**
FAVORITE TOY:	**Extra-special orange juice carton**
MOTTO:	**"Don't be jeally of my jelly."**
LIFE DREAM:	**To win a break-dancing contest**

MEET

Cheesy!

Cheesy loves pizza. Looooooooves pizza. Cheesy once got caught in the washing machine on the spin cycle because he spotted a pair of pizza-patterned pajama pants crammed inside and thought he was about to be the only customer at an all-you-can eat, PERSONAL PIZZA BUFFET. Sure, he's gone through some ups and downs in his quest for pizza, but nothing keeps Cheesy down for long. His dreams are full of pepperoni trees and his paws are prepped for pizza picking!

LIKES: Pizza, calzones
DISLIKES: Empty pizza boxes
FAVORITE SNACK: Supreme salmon pizza with anchovies
HOBBIES: Stalking pizza delivery kitties
FAVORITE TOY: Catnip cactus
MOTTO: "Grab life by the slice."
LIFE DREAM: To live in a house made of pizza

MEET

Snoozer!

#IFIFITS

SERIES 1

Snoozer begins her day with a nice mug of coffee brewed just the way she likes it: steamy enough to warm her belly fur as she settles down onto the cup. After a light six-hour snooze, she settles into the real R.E.M. relaxation as the clock strikes noon. The afternoon brings on the more rigorous catnapping: there are dream birds to catch, dream scents to sniff, and dream sounds to hear. After a full day, she usually hits the cat bed early and is out like a light. It's hard work, but SOMEBODY'S GOTTA SNOOZE IT!

LIKES: Dreams about breakfast food
DISLIKES: Daylight savings time
FAVORITE SNACK: Catnip blend coffee
HOBBIES: Sleeping, napping, snoring, drooling
FAVORITE TOY: Wind-up mouse
MOTTO: "Give a cat a nap and she'll snoozle 4 a day. Teach a cat 2 nap and she'll snoozle for LIFE."
LIFE DREAM: To live in her very own cat café

MEET

Ocho!

MEOWGIC

SERIES 2

Ocho has distraction down to an art. It doesn't help that she spends most of the time behind the computer. This cream-colored kitty is the digital design queen, and her photography skills are top-notch. She can alter a photo to make it look like forty kitties are standing on each other's heads, to make two kitties look like they swapped tails, and even erase kitties from photographs in the blink of an eye. Her work is so **MEOWSTERFUL** that some of her photos show her walking around on more than four paws. But it has to be **FURTO-SHOPPED**! I mean, who ever heard of a kitty with eight paws? Did Ocho just wink?

LIKES: Graphic design
DISLIKES: Unwanted attention
FAVORITE SNACK: Gingersnaps
HOBBIES: Taking photos, editing photos, running marathons
FAVORITE TOY: Magic 8 ball
MOTTO: "Ur eyez are doin a deceive."
LIFE DREAM: To figure out how to regrow the rest of her legs

MEET

Reach!

Yes, Reach is tall. No, he doesn't play basketball. Yes, he knows he would be great at basketball. Anyway, Reach doesn't think that he's *that* tall; it's more that the other kitties are so short. Sure, his paws seem to lengthen when he's leaning to grab a glass of milk on the very top shelf, and his body can appear longer when he's helping a kitty out of a tree. But Reach isn't **MEOWGICAL**—just flexible...

LIKES: Helping out the other kitties
DISLIKES: Basketball
FAVORITE SNACK: Pringles
HOBBIES: Rescuing lost kittens from trees, dusting those hard-to-see places
FAVORITE TOY: Silly string
MOTTO: "I iz not tall. I iz vertically blessed."
LIFE DREAM: To become a FUR-TASTIC firefighter—he doesn't even need the ladder!

MEET Meowlin!

By day, a **MEOWGICIAN** at a family restaurant geared toward kittens. By night, the greatest Dungeons & Dragons **DUNGEON-MEOWSTER** on four paws. Meowlin might get his robes tugged on by unruly kittens all day when he's at Meowgic Manny's Pizza Palace, but when he leaves work, he's the king of the wizards. With his own **PURR-SONALIZED** board and eight sets of dice, he's ready to make the **MEOWGIC** happen. No kitty is sure if the beard is part of his **CAT-STUME** or if he's just a very old kitty—either way, he's never been seen without it!

LIKES: Twelve-hour D&D MEOW-A-THONS
DISLIKES: Mornings
FAVORITE SNACK: Pop Rocks
HOBBIES: Swishing his robe around
FAVORITE TOY: His PAW-THENTIC gold wand
MOTTO: "Leave room 4 meowgic!"
LIFE DREAM: To invent his own expansion pack for Dungeons & Dragons

#MEOWGIC
SERIES 2

Viktor can fly. No, really. He never met his **PAW-RENTS**, but rumor has it they both had wings the size of puppies and could soar through the air. Viktor wasn't born with wings, but he knows that is just an irrelevant detail. Although his test flights haven't gone well so far, Viktor knows that's only because he hasn't found the right way to calibrate his custom cardboard flying **CAT-TRAPTION**. But it's only a matter of time until he's hitting the sky just like his **PAW-RENTS** did, and watching his own fur fly!

LIKES: Lightweight cardboard
DISLIKES: Interfering squirrels
FAVORITE SNACK: Red Bull
HOBBIES: Tinkering with flight PURR-OTOTYPES
FAVORITE TOY: His trusty cardboard box with aerodynamic flaps
MOTTO: "I iz one wiff dah sky."
LIFE DREAM: To really fly with his own four paws

FUR-EVER HUNGRY!

MEET Chomp!

NOMZ

SERIES 1

Chomp is a sweet little kitty with eyes bigger than her stomach. But watch her closely, because she might not be able to finish what's on her plate, but she sure likes to taste everything on the table. She always asks permission to eat your food, but she isn't really listening to the answer. Cheeky Chomp is going to take a bite, no matter what! When she's not nibbling on nearby snacks, she's perfecting her hot sauce recipe for her absolute FUR-VORITE snack: TACOS!

LIKES: Biting, gnawing, nibbling

DISLIKES: Hearing "no"

FAVORITE SNACK: Tacos, taco salad, taquitos

HOBBIES: Testing hot sauces, chomp-chomp-chomping

FAVORITE TOY: Purple wand toy

MOTTO: "Eating iz the answer, no matter dah question!"

LIFE DREAM: To be placed inside a taco the size of MEOWXICO and eat her way out

MEET Loafy!

#NOMZ SERIES 1

Lovable Loafy loves toast the most—if only he could find out where his last piece went! With big eyes for spotting snacks and a long tongue for licking extra crumbs out of his fur, Loafy's best **FURRIEND** is food. Sure, he bumps into things a lot, but no pain, **NO GRAIN**! Whether he's whiskers-deep in some yummy bread, or looking for his next snack, Loafy never has a care in the world.

LIKES:	Bread, toast, toasty bread, breaded toast
DISLIKES:	Gluten-free food
FAVORITE SNACK:	French toast
HOBBIES:	Eating bread, thinking about bread, making sand statues
FAVORITE TOY:	Pink teacup
MOTTO:	"Everything iz food if u eat it!"
LIFE DREAM:	To judge a bread-baking competition

MEET Stuffs!

#NOMZ SERIES 1

Stuffs doesn't just love food, he's a food **A-FUR-CIONADO**. He has expensive taste, and only samples the very best fish and milk that restaurants have to offer. His **REPAWTATION** as a food critic is renowned, and chefs are always trying to impress him with their latest masterpieces. Little do they know, Stuffs has a secret love of French fries, and has a deal with the manager at **MEOWCDONALD**'s that lets him sneak in at midnight for a large order of extra-salty fries washed down with a **DIET ICED FLEA**.

LIKES:	Filet mignon, caviar, liver pâté
DISLIKES:	Poor manners
FAVORITE SNACK:	MEOWCDONALD's French fries
HOBBIES:	Eating food, judging food, writing about food
FAVORITE TOY:	Fluffy bib
MOTTO:	"If French fries be the food of love, nom on!"
LIFE DREAM:	To own his own five-star restaurant

MEET

Chunks!

#NOMZ  SERIES 1

Chunks has double the fun with food; the first time she eats it, and then when it comes back up! Queen of the hairballs, she loves anything gross and gruesome, and you'll often find her chuckling after hacking up some funky fur! Grinning green Chunks is never afraid to get her paws dirty, but she often skips cleanup—just because. She's extra-competitive, and always aims her hairballs at the trash to go for a **SLAM CHUNK!** Nailed it.

LIKES: Hairballs, puke, boogers, dirt
DISLIKES: Baths
FAVORITE SNACK: Twice-digested turkey
HOBBIES: Hairball hacky sack, digging in the yard
FAVORITE TOY: Red cup
MOTTO: "Food iz even better dah second time around!"
LIFE DREAM: To set a world record for biggest hairball ever coughed up

MEET

Bowley!

#NOMZ SERIES 1

It might seem like Bowley is in that fish bowl voluntarily, but it was actually court-ordered. The last time he got out of the bowl, he was found swimming in the dolphin tank at the **MEOW-TERAY AQUARIUM** trying to eat a pod of dolphins that were easily ten times his size. It took five aquarium employees to get him out of the tank. Bowley is really an easygoing kitty, he just has a lot of feelings about seafood. A **LOT** of feelings.

LIKES: Shrimp, krill, anchovies, eels, tuna, salmon, swordfish, squid
DISLIKES: Getting caught
FAVORITE SNACK: Dolphin (if he ever gets to try it)
HOBBIES: Taking bubble bowl baths
FAVORITE TOY: Yellow brush
MOTTO: "I iz gonna need a bigger bowl!"
LIFE DREAM: To have his lifetime ban from the MEOW-TARAY AQUARIUM lifted

EAT. PURR. REPEAT.

MEET Totes!

SERIES 2

Clean up on aisle cute! Totes's eyes are as big as his stomach, and he's always on the hunt for new things to munch on. Totes loves to taste different NOMZ from all over the globe, and so you'll always find him in the grocery store ready to slip into some kitty's cart. If you're not careful, you won't notice his wide eyes until they're staring up at you from the inside of an empty grocery bag, followed by an UNKITTYLIKE burp.

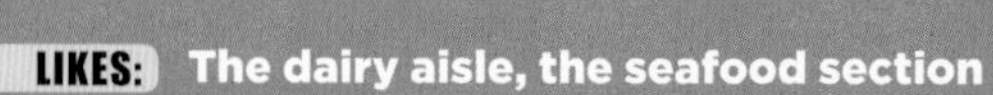

LIKES: The dairy aisle, the seafood section
DISLIKES: Well-sealed snacks
FAVORITE SNACK: Sample-size cheese cubes
HOBBIES: Grazing at the grocery, hiding
FAVORITE TOY: Cardboard cat scratcher
MOTTO: "Iz u gonna finish dat?"
LIFE DREAM: To travel to FURRANCE for a food tour

MEET
Tubby Tubz!

#NOMZ

SERIES 2

Tubby Tubz has paws. The other kitties are sure of it. They've just never seen them in action. Tubby Tubz loves to loaf, paws tucked, and he seems to appear places as if by **MEOWGIC** instead of walking. Although his sister Snoozer loves to sleep, Tubby Tubz is always wide-awake, on the hunt for some bread to sink his teeth into. Since he looks so much like a loaf already, he usually only gets caught after he's **PAW-LISHED** off three or four bags of pumpernickel and rye.

LIKES: The smell of a brioche bun
DISLIKES: Locked breadboxes
FAVORITE SNACK: Garlic bread
HOBBIES: Baguette fencing, bagel tossing
FAVORITE TOY: Green bread clip from his first twelve-grain loaf
MOTTO: "Free bread. Nuff said."
LIFE DREAM: To have a loaf named after himself at the local bakery

JUST
LOAFIN' AROUND

MEET
Stackz!

#NOMZ

SERIES 2

Breakfast is the most **IMPURRTENT** meal of the day, and Stackz makes breakfast last all day long. She starts her morning with a tall glass of milk followed by seventeen strips of tuna bacon. She washes those down with a huge helping of **EGGS OVER CHEESY**, and then it's on to the main event: pancakes as far as the eye can see! Chocolate-chip catnip pancakes, mackerel pancakes slathered in marmalade, syrupy salmon pancakes with a whipped cream topping. **PURR-FECT**!

LIKES: Breakfast, brunch, brinner
DISLIKES: Wasting time with lunch and dinner
FAVORITE SNACK: Mahi-mahi pancakes with strawberry milk
HOBBIES: PAW-FECTING her pancake toss
FAVORITE TOY: Purple spatula
MOTTO: "Why breakfast, when u can breakslow?"
LIFE DREAM: To publish a breakfast food cookbook

MEET
Beau Loney!

NOMZ

SERIES 2

Some kitties say that Beau Loney has crazy eyes, but he's just **PAWSSIONATE** about lunch meat, that's all. Sandwiches are his **FUR-VORITE**, but he'll take anything he doesn't have to make himself. When he's **FELINE** extra sneaky, he tricks other kitties into feeding him, gobbles the meal in one bite, and runs off, giggling! But Beau Loney's only weakness is baloney, and he can be easily trapped by a tall baloney sandwich. Then, the other kitties make him wash the dishes as revenge for his snack attacks.

LIKES: PAWSTRAMI, roast beef, baloney
DISLIKES: Cooking
FAVORITE SNACK: Baloney sandwich with anchovies and pickle chips, stacked as high as his head
HOBBIES: Turning on the kittycat eyes to get free sandwiches
FAVORITE TOY: Blue feathery wand
MOTTO: "Iz not personal. Iz baloney."
LIFE DREAM: To hire a private chef to make him sandwiches daily

MEET
Olga!

NOMZ

SERIES 2

Olga firmly believes in the idea that food should be an **ADVENTURE**. Never one to shy away from anything edible, she'll try the zaniest, craziest, kookiest meals without a second thought! Fried grasshopper? She's had hundreds. Pickled eggs? Delicious! Frog legs? More, please! Olga doesn't just love the taste of food, she loves the smell of it, and so when the last bite is eaten, she doesn't just "lick the bowl," she gets **INSIDE THE BOWL**. This fearless foodie always has her eyes glued to the Cooking Channel, usually still inside a bowl of whatever she just finished eating!

LIKES: Cooking shows like "MEOWSTERCHEF" and "CAT-THROAT KITCHEN"
DISLIKES: Commercials
FAVORITE SNACK: Fried tarantulas
HOBBIES: Shouting at the TV during competitive cooking shows, testing out odd concoctions in the kitchen
FAVORITE TOY: White spinning top
MOTTO: "Life iz short. Lick dah bowl."
LIFE DREAM: To compete (and win) on a reality cooking show

MEET
Noperz!

#NOTFELINEIT

SERIES 1

Noperz isn't negative, he's **REALISTIC**. It takes more than a little catnip to impress him. He hates the flash of the laser light, rolls his eyes at the feathery fuzz of wand toys, and is absolutely bored to tears by the sight of a scratching post. Noperz is his own kitty, and when the other silly kittens are cheering over tuna, you'll find him solemnly eating kibble, swearing that it tastes better than the juiciest steak. It's not that he's stubborn; he just needs to do things his own way. Always. Or **ELSE**.

LIKES: Solitude
DISLIKES: Conforming, silly toys, silly kitties
FAVORITE SNACK: Any store-brand kibble
HOBBIES: Judging, glaring, sniffing in disdain
FAVORITE TOY: As if!
MOTTO: "Prepare for dah worst. Expect dah worst. DAH END."
LIFE DREAM: To be left alone

MEET
Flakes!

SERIES 1

Fabulous Flakes always has the last word when it comes to **FUR-SHION**. A retired model with an eye for making kitty paws pop, all Flakes has to do is break out her famous icy stare to stop **ANYKITTY** in their tracks. Flakes hates jokes—laughing gives her wrinkle lines—but whenever she walks into the room, you can bet she'll be posing. Sure, nowadays she only designs high-end sweaters for the kitty elite, but she can still strut the catwalk better than any other.

LIKES: VERPAWCE, KATE SPAYED, PURRADA
DISLIKES: Coupons
FAVORITE SNACK: Quinoa
HOBBIES: Designing, modeling
FAVORITE TOY: Sewing MEWCHINE
MOTTO: "It's called fur-shion. Look it up."
LIFE DREAM: To create a line of luxury CLAWTHING

MEET
Niles!

No kitty is quite sure where Niles comes from, but he has a funny accent and puts a lot of tea in his milk. **FUR-OCIOUSLY** independent, Niles is the kind of kitty who will put a can of tuna out for you only to bat it off the counter while maintaining unblinking eye contact. A **MEOWSTER** at chess, Niles loves challenging other kitties to a match just to knock down their pawns one by one. His eyes don't miss a move, and before the other kitties know it, their king has lost all nine of his lives. Checkmate!

LIKES: Pushing things to the ground
DISLIKES: Losing
FAVORITE SNACK: Crumpets
HOBBIES: Chess, cricket, gardening
FAVORITE TOY: Monogrammed chessboard
MOTTO: "Keep calm and haz a cup of tea."
LIFE DREAM: To win a worldwide chess tournament

MEET
Flufferton!

NOTFELINEIT
SERIES 1

Flufferton is so over the humidity. Maintaining her luscious locks takes a lot of energy, and she's ready for a catnap. Every morning starts with fish-scented fur serums in the shower, followed by whisker moisturizer and some careful coiffing with her specially made hair dryer. She spends a good six hours every day getting her fluff just right. It's a lot of work to look this fierce, but Flufferton knows the other kitties expect **PURR-FECTION**, so she'll just have to keep serving looks!

LIKES: Anything with argan oil
DISLIKES: Dandruff
FAVORITE SNACK: Mango body butter
HOBBIES: Shampooing, straightening, curling
FAVORITE TOY: The Fluffinator 3000 (her hair dryer)
MOTTO: "Ask not what ur fluff can do 4 u, ask what u can do 4 ur fluff!"
LIFE DREAM: To have 365 good hair days in a row

MEET
Tourist Tom!

#NOTFELINEIT

SERIES 2

Tourist Tom has lost his luggage so many times that he has the personal cell phone numbers of four different pilots who work for JETMEW AIRLINES. He can't help it—bad luck follows him like a flea. He once got such a bad FUR-BURN on an island off the coast of MEOWXICO that he was shedding red for a month. He's afraid of heights, flights, water, adventures, bugs, strangers, and his own teeny tail. So why does he always find himself on another new trip, wearing nothing but the clothes the airline gave him from the Lost & Found?

LIKES: Traveling
DISLIKES: Traveling
FAVORITE SNACK: Airplane peanuts
HOBBIES: Almost-dying, almost-diving, getting lost
FAVORITE TOY: His super-safe scuba goggles
MOTTO: "Kittehs who can, do. Kittehs who can't, tour."
LIFE DREAM: To finish just one of his vacations without disaster

MEET
Mr. Meh!

#NOTFELINEIT

SERIES 2

Actually, don't meet Mr. Meh. He'd prefer you didn't. Please go back the way you came, that's it, just back out sloooowly, and keep walking. Mr. Meh has been around FUR-EVER, and has seen the world. He just didn't find it all that compelling, and would like it to leave him alone, thank you very much. He's one grumpy kitty, and when he's not griping about the weather, the other kitties, his CARPAL TAIL SYNDROME, and the general state of the universe, he's asleep. MEH!

LIKES: To be left alone
DISLIKES: Getting up
FAVORITE SNACK: Water
HOBBIES: Complaining, taking rage naps
FAVORITE TOY: Stuffed animal porcupine
MOTTO: "Ready, set, NO!"
LIFE DREAM: To have one moment of peace

MEET
Jacket!

Oh. My. Whiskers. Jacket hates getting her fur cut, and for good reason—CAT-HAIRSTYLISTS are always messing up her beautiful green coat! First, she contracted super-forceful Finnish fleas after coming in for a quick shampoo and they had to shave her from ears to tail. Then when her hair grew back, Pants pranked her with his most potent itching powder and she scratched it all back off! And the last time she went in for a trim she left the salon looking like a total hot mess. You've got to be KITTEN me!

LIKES: Sweaters, flea shampoo
DISLIKES: Fur-cuts
FAVORITE SNACK: Shaved ice
HOBBIES: Moisturizing, entering experimental hair growth trials
FAVORITE TOY: Red cat dancer
MOTTO: "Dis fur won't purr!"
LIFE DREAM: To start a NON-PURROFIT for balding kitties

MEET
Sid!

#NOTFELINEIT
SERIES 2

It took anxious Sid ten years to graduate from college because he couldn't decide on what his major should be. First, he was a math major, but CAT-CULUS class knocked him on his tail. He even tested out MEOWSICAL THEATER, but he can't carry a tune to save any of his nine lives. Sid ended up picking FUR-LOSOPHY at random, and now spends his days thinking. Thinking about his next step. And thinking about everything that could go wrong. And—uh oh.

LIKES: Having a plan
DISLIKES: Making a plan
FAVORITE SNACK: Nutella pancakes
HOBBIES: Worrying, stressing, imagining
FAVORITE TOY: Purple laser light—no, blue treat ball—no, cardboard scratching post! Oh no.
MOTTO: "I think, therefore I iz confused."
LIFE DREAM: To make a five-year plan (okay, three-year plan? Maybe two-year plan...)

 # PURRBLISS

NOTHING STRESSES MEOWT

MEET Maxalax!

 # PURRBLISS

SERIES 2

Maxalax has got the skill of chill. Rumor has it he started out as a stockbroker in MEW YORK but quit after a stressful day, poured milk all over his desk, and hightailed it out the door. Nowadays, Maxalax spends his time weeding his catnip garden, getting deep-tissue whisker massages, and soaking his fur in the sauna at the spa. Between listening to mellow MEOWSIC and dozing on his hammock, Maxalax always lets the GOOD TIMES PURR.

LIKES: Reggae, 600-thread count sheets

DISLIKES: Stress

FAVORITE SNACK: PAW-PSICLES

HOBBIES: Falling asleep outside, table tennis

FAVORITE TOY: Green beanbag chair

MOTTO: "Monday, Tuesday, Wednesday, Thursday, Friday, Saturday, SPA DAY!"

LIFE DREAM: To move to the white sand beaches of MEOWI, Hawaii, and never look back

MEET Mick Meower!

Mick Meower tends to lose himself in the power of the jam. His tail can wail on the guitar for hours at a time, and he usually forgets where he is when the strings start to sing. A certified rock star that's in it for the **MEOWSIC**, not the fame, Mick Meower nevertheless has die-hard fans. He only plays small shows with his band, **THE MEW**, but fans still find out and pack the place. He's got no choice but to rock his paws off!

LIKES: Snacks, hugs, and rock 'n roll
DISLIKES: Selling out
FAVORITE SNACK: Apple pie
HOBBIES: Wailing on his guitar, writing songs, practicing his rock star face
FAVORITE TOY: His pink electric guitar, Thunder
MOTTO: "We built this kitty on rock 'n roll!"
LIFE DREAM: To go down in rock 'n roll HISS-TORY

MEET Chewy!

PURRBLISS

SERIES 2

Chewy is allergic to everything. She has lactose intolerance, gluten intolerance, best-snacks-ever intolerance. She loves all food with her entire tiny tummy, but it does not love her back. Chewy's incredibly stealthy, and she can sneak French fries, nab nacho cheese, and guzzle down whole milk whenever **ANYKITTY'S** back is turned. But she always gets caught in the end when her allergies give her uncontrollable hairballs! Chewy's cute, but her snacking habits are a mess!

LIKES: Anything with dairy, gluten, nuts, or salt
DISLIKES: Anything with dairy, gluten, nuts, or salt
FAVORITE SNACK: French fries dipped in chipotle mayo
HOBBIES: Scoping out new foods, sneaking snacks
FAVORITE TOY: Empty French-fry carton
MOTTO: "Worth it."
LIFE DREAM: To find a cure for food allergies

MEET

Munch!

\# PURRBLISS

SERIES 2

Munch hosts an exclusive game night in town. It requires four PAW-SSWORDS and a pair of personalized dice just to get in the cat-door! But once you're in, snacks are the key to getting Munch to welcome you with open paws. She's a nationally ranked board game champion, but snacks make her cards twitch and her shuffles go wonky. She once lost a heated tournament of SNIFFERS OF CAT-AN that had been going on for sixteen hours because someone dangled a particularly nice bag of cheese curls in front of her nose. Yahtzee!

LIKES: Chips, cookies, pretzels, candy
DISLIKES: Cheaters
FAVORITE SNACK: Mice cakes
HOBBIES: Learning trick shuffles, PURR-FECTING her poker face, PAW-NOPOLY practice rounds
FAVORITE TOY: Blue squeaky bird
MOTTO: "No dice, no snackz."
LIFE DREAM: To invent her own board game

MEET

Sir Stinks-a-lot!

Sir Stinks-a-lot has made it his mission to collect the most fragrant items he can find. His nose delights in the smelliest of smells, and you can often find him whiskers-deep in the heart of the laundry hamper, taking a big whiff of old gym clothes and sweaty socks. The other kitties give him a wide berth on laundry day, but Sir Stinks-a-lot doesn't mind—he's just glad to be able to sneak a sniff, especially if that sniff reeks of rotten tuna and spoiled milk!

SERIES 2

LIKES: Mildew, mold, body odor
DISLIKES: Flowers
FAVORITE SNACK: Limburger cheese
HOBBIES: Sorting socks, folding clothes, digging through the trash
FAVORITE TOY: Lucky gym sock with the stain on the heel
MOTTO: "Stop and smell the toes-ez!"
LIFE DREAM: To make his own perfume

MEET

Prickle Paws!

Prickle Paws has a long list of **FUR-BIAS**. She's afraid of mice, storms, dogs, sudden moves, not-so-sudden moves, loud sounds, soft sounds, kitchen appliances, cars, mops, UNICORNS, and most of all, her little sister Sketch. But Prickle Paws doesn't like to show her soft and fluffy side, so when she gets a little spooked, she puts the **GLARE IN HER TAIL** and the stomp in her step and hisses with all her might! Take that, unicorns!

#SCAREDYCATS

SERIES 1

LIKES: Silence
DISLIKES: Unicorns
FAVORITE SNACK: Prickly pears
HOBBIES: Hissing, spitting, licking the prickles out of her fur
FAVORITE TOY: Green rubber ball
MOTTO: "Dah only thing we haz to fear iz EVERYTHING."
LIFE DREAM: To frighten her fears right back!

MEET

Peekerz!

Peekerz has been studying **CAT-SPIRACY** theories for years, and she's started to get a little **PAW-RANOID**. It's been months since any of the kitties have caught a glimpse of Peekerz out of her box—she stays safely surrounded by cardboard as she keeps an eye out for anything fishy. Practice makes perfect, and Peekerz has been spying for so long that she's got dirt on every single kitty. They've got to be careful, or their secrets will be snatched up by a certain scaredy-cat spy!

LIKES: Boxes, gossip
DISLIKES: Wide open spaces
FAVORITE SNACK: Stockpiled ramen noodles
HOBBIES: Spying, sneaking, eavesdropping
FAVORITE TOY: Her sturdiest brown box
MOTTO: "Life is like a box of Peekerz. U never know what I iz gonna hear!"
LIFE DREAM: To find the truth for every CAT-SPIRACY theory out there

MEET
Specks!

#SCAREDYCATS

SERIES 1

Specks is **NOT AN ALIEN**. Definitely not. He's just green with enormous eyes, and sometimes he forgets the names of obvious things . . . like trees, or milk, or birds. Also, he has a hard time with fruit . . . something about bananas really confuses him. But that's only because he was a shelter kitty, and he hasn't seen much of the big wide world! Specks may never lose that look of pure shock on his face, but maybe after a while he'll stop whispering into that recording device late at night in what sounds like a different language.

LIKES: Earth
DISLIKES: Technological malfunctions
FAVORITE SNACK: Regular kitty food that kitties like
HOBBIES: Being a totally normal kitty, reporting back to headquarters
FAVORITE TOY: "Stuffed" alien mouse
MOTTO: "Meow, am I right, guys?"
LIFE DREAM: To catch his tail (and not the one the galactic government sent after him)

MEET
Drizzle!

#SCAREDYCATS

SERIES 1

Drizzle is always dripping because he's a constantly taking **EMERGENCY BATHS**. It's not that he's scared of germs, it's just he's constantly gripped with the inescapable horror that they're everywhere and on everything. Drizzle once downed a whole bottle of bubble mix because he thought it was just super-clean soap and farted bubbles for three days. This kitty is so **SQUEAKY-CLEAN** that even his hairballs come out combed.

LIKES: Bubble baths
DISLIKES: Dirt, bacteria, microscopic germs
FAVORITE SNACK: Toothpaste
HOBBIES: Showering, bathing, taking quick ten-hour sink soaks

FAVORITE TOY: Yellow toy boat
MOTTO: "Cleanlinezz iz next to catlinezz!"
LIFE DREAM: To invent a portable bath machine

MEET
Chippy!

WOKEUPLIKETHIS

SERIES 2

Oops! Did the milk spill? Did the glass holding the milk shatter? Did the part of the floor that the glass fell on suddenly cave in? It's not Chippy's fault! He's just isn't exactly what you'd call **CAT-ORDINATED**. Chippy once broke a bulletproof window just by knocking on it—his fluff is as tough as fluff can be! Chippy woke up clumsy, but he works it. Sure, he trips a lot, but he always lands on his feet. And his super-cute floof paired with big **KITTY-CAT** eyes let him get away with even the most crumbled cookies!

LIKES: Bubble wrap, helmets
DISLIKES: Fragile things like eggs, glass, steel
FAVORITE SNACK: KIT-CAT BARS
HOBBIES: Mice hockey, Kung-Fu PAWRATE
FAVORITE TOY: Blocks
MOTTO: "If it ain't broke, break it!"
LIFE DREAM: To be a black belt in PAWRATE

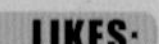

MEET
Cubbie!

#WOKEUPLIKETHIS

SERIES 2

Cubbie is the Queen of Cozy. She loves to squeeze herself into the tightest spots, because what's a snuggle without a whole lot of SNUG? Rumor has it that Cubbie was born right in her favorite blue box, and so she just stretched her little paws and stayed. Sometimes all you'll see of Cubbie are her whiskers, but she's been known to spook the SCAREDY-KITTIES by peeking a nose out of her hiding spot. Cubbie just wants to cuddle, but doesn't understand that other kitties sometimes feel CAT-STROPHOBIC in teeny spaces!

LIKES: Crawlspaces, dumbwaiters, gaps in couch cushions
DISLIKES: Feeling exposed
FAVORITE SNACK: Mini MARSHMEOWS
HOBBIES: Hiding, peeking, sneaking
FAVORITE TOY: Yellow yarn mouse
MOTTO: "I iz gonna offer u a snuggle u can't refuse."
LIFE DREAM: To move into a tiny house

MEET
Snoozin' Suzan!

Snoozin' Suzan used to just be called Suzan, but whenever ANYKITTY tries to get her to do anything, she's well...she's snoozing. She can't help it! The couch is so inviting, and that laptop has just the right level of warmth for her tummy, and that pointy rock looks like it has good catnap potential. Okay, so she's not picky about where she snoozes, but the most IMPURR-TENT thing is that she gets twenty-three hours of sleep a day like any good, healthy kitty should.

#WOKEUPLIKETHIS

SERIES 2

LIKES: Dreaming about naps
DISLIKES: Being called Suzie (DO. NOT. CALL HER SUZIE!)
FAVORITE SNACK: Peanut butter on anything
HOBBIES: Dozing, drifting, drooling
FAVORITE TOY: Stuffed animal kitty with only three paws (it's a TRI-PAWD)
MOTTO: "It's snooze-o'-clock somewhere!"
LIFE DREAM: To set the world record for longest nap ever taken

MEET
Chimi!

Born in the heart of **CAT-HAIRIZONA**, Chimi goes wild over any Tex-Mex food she can get her paws on. She's not shy and she's extra-tiny, so you'll see her pop up in the unlikeliest of places—like in the middle of your burrito. What, you didn't want a **PURRITO**? Chimi's favorite look is a wrap (a tortilla wrap), but she's versatile: you'll also find her lying flat in pizza boxes, nestled in Chinese takeout containers, and sipping from the opposite end of the straw at the bottom of your milkshake!

LIKES: Eating fast food, hiding in fast food, being fast food

DISLIKES: Running out of things to munch on

FAVORITE SNACK: Chimichangas, of course!

HOBBIES: Fashioning tortilla togas, salsa dancing (literally)

FAVORITE TOY: The littlest lettuce leaf

MOTTO: "U iz what u eat! Hopefully..."

LIFE DREAM: To win a lifetime supply of food from PAW-CO BELL

MEET
Fwed!

If need-be, Fwed can disappear in thirty seconds flat, and you'd never see tail nor whisker of him ever again. This kitty is as cute as can be—when his eye isn't twitching. No kitty knows why Fwed is **PAWPARING** so diligently for disaster, but this pawranoid kitty has a safe room, a secret bunker with enough milk to last a year, and a panic pillow he keeps wrapped around him at all times. He sleeps with one eye open, and is always ready to vanish in plain sight at **THE DROP OF A CAT**. Wait—where'd he go?

LIKES: Safety precautions

DISLIKES: Unpredictable weather patterns

FAVORITE SNACK: Army-issued rations

HOBBIES: Daily disaster drills, MEOWGIC tricks

FAVORITE TOY: Bright orange panic pillow

MOTTO: "Iz I pawranoid? Or iz I just pawpared?"

LIFE DREAM: To escape the doom that awaits us all

#WORKINIT

FELINE GOOD!

MEET Meowzart!

#WORKINIT

When Meowzart puts her paws to the keys, even the grumpiest kitties get a case of the feels. Queen of the DANCE PAW-TY, Meowzart has had music in her heart FUR-EVER—she even took her first steps on the keys of a piano! This kitty can't leave home without her keyboard, and she's always ready to throw down the PURR-FECT beat for her friends. She might keep her eyes closed, but Meowzart never misses a note!

LIKES: Making MEOWSIC
DISLIKES: Charades
FAVORITE SNACK: TUNE-A fish
HOBBIES: Composing, making playlists, getting PAW-DICURES
FAVORITE TOY: Wireless headphones
MOTTO: "Meow like no one'z watching!"
LIFE DREAM: To have 10 albums streaming on PAW-TIFY

MEET
Francis!

Francis is a no-nonsense kitty who brings home the milk. None of the kitties know exactly what he does, but it involves numbers, and faxes, and something about quarterly reports. Francis is as uptight as his tie, but rumor has it that on **CATURDAYS** he wears jeans. No kitty has seen it for themselves, but Francis has to relax now and then, doesn't he? In the meantime, he's all business. Now, hold his calls!

LIKES: Pocket protectors
DISLIKES: Tardiness
FAVORITE SNACK: Microwaveable soup
HOBBIES: Hole-punching, pencil-sharpening, data entry
FAVORITE TOY: Red stapler
MOTTO: "Don't be busy. Be paw-ductive."
LIFE DREAM: To become the Chief Executive PAWFFICER, C.E.P.

MEET
Captain Kitteh!

WORKINIT
SERIES 1

By day, Captain Kitteh is a **CLAWMIC** book-loving supernerd, and by night, she's . . . okay, so she's not that different at night, BUT she's ready, willing, and able to fight crime! She hasn't gotten a call yet from any kittens stuck in trees, but she'll be waiting. Okay, so sometimes she falls asleep waiting, but constant vigilance is hard when you fight video game zombie-cats for six hours and drink your weight in whole milk! She's working on it.

LIKES: Clawmic books, superhero movies
DISLIKES: Waiting
FAVORITE SNACK: Chili cheese fries
HOBBIES: Playing video games, reading clawmics
FAVORITE TOY: Purple superhero helmet
MOTTO: "Wherever there are kittenz in trees, u will find me. Whenever the milk haz run out, I'll be there."
LIFE DREAM: To be so well known that kitties actually try to find out her secret identity

MEET
Professor Purrkins!

The **FURRIENDLIEST** mad scientist you'll ever meet, Professor Purrkins is a happy-go-lucky kitty with a **PAWHD** in Biochemistry. When he's not poring over old books and learning about Ancient Egyptian kitty curses and rituals, he's in his laboratory, trying to grow his own milk out of thin air! Professor Purrkins can get so lost in his work and not come up for milk for weeks at a time. But despite his big brain, he still can't seem to invent something that'll keep his glasses from sliding down his face.

WORKINIT

SERIES 1

LIKES: The PAWTHAGOREAN Theorem, the PURR-IODIC Table of Elements
DISLIKES: Being interrupted in the middle of an experiment
FAVORITE SNACK: Ants on a log
HOBBIES: Reading, mixing chemicals
FAVORITE TOY: Orange clipboard
MOTTO: "Purr-eka! I've solved it!"
LIFE DREAM: To grow milk in a lab

MEET
Eugene!

WORKINIT

SERIES 1

Eugene is the king of cool. With his trusty **FEN-PURR** bass always strapped to his side and his sunglasses perched on the tip his nose, he always looks like he's about to say, "Yeah. And?" Eugene doesn't say much; he lets his bass do the **MEOWING**, and always lays down a funky line for the kitties to groove to. After a long show he likes to kick back with a chocolate milk on the rocks and listen to the smooth sounds of some of his favorite soul cats.

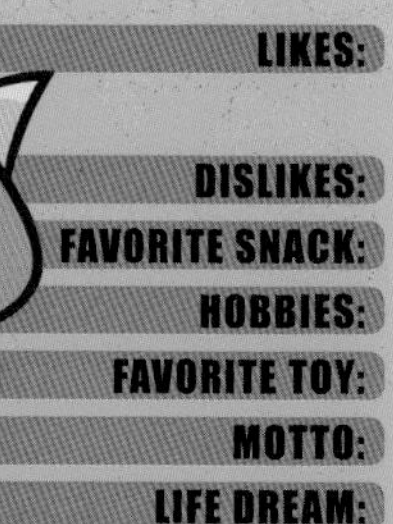

LIKES: Rocking out to EARTH, WIND, & FUR and THE RED HOT KITTY PEPPERS
DISLIKES: Microphone feedback
FAVORITE SNACK: Soul food
HOBBIES: Listening to MEOWSIC, jamming on his bass
FAVORITE TOY: Blue catnip music note
MOTTO: "Iz all about dah chill."
LIFE DREAM: To play bass for a packed stadium of fans

#WORKINIT

IT'S MEOW OR NEVER!

MEET
Sparkle Time!

What time is it? It's SPARKLE TIME! Or, at least she thinks it is...the clock is looking extra-blurry today for some reason. Sparkle Time doesn't need glasses; she just wears them because they're so in **RIGHT MEOW**. Sure, several doctors told her that if she doesn't wear them at all times she could end up in a **CLAWFUL ACCIDENT**, but that's just silly talk! Sparkle Time is the peppiest kitty you'll ever meet. She plans **PAWTIES** for her fellow kitties, and her soirees are nothing short of sparkling. Every. Single. Time. *Sparkle Time*!

LIKES: Glitter, confetti, rainbow streamers
DISLIKES: Foggy nights, contact lenses
FAVORITE SNACK: Cake Pops
HOBBIES: PAWTY planning, scrapbooking
FAVORITE TOY: Hot pink glitter pen
MOTTO: "Iz alwayz time to sparkle!"
LIFE DREAM: To open her own PAWTY-planning business

SERIES 2

Zenny is always on the move, and this CAT-TORTIONIST can bend into shapes that don't seem PAWSIBLE! His schedule is chock-full of kitties ready to get their sweat on, and he makes them work for their tuna with his intense CATZ-ER-CISE class followed by Step AERO-LICKS and hot yoga. Zenny is a tough fluff to work with, because he expects the very best and won't PAWSE until he gets it! Kitties cry wolf every day, saying they're going to quit, but every morning they're back in class, tails ready to twist. Five, six, seven, eight!

LIKES: Punctuality
DISLIKES: Quitters
FAVORITE SNACK: CLAWTTAGE cheese on toast
HOBBIES: Dancing, prancing, stretching
FAVORITE TOY: Black and red yoga mat
MOTTO: "No kitteh iz purr-fect. But we can try."
LIFE DREAM: To build an exercise studio where he can teach his classes

MEET

Len!

WORKINIT

SERIES 2

Len is always dressed in his best. After all, you never know when you're going to go to the **PAWPERA** to catch a show, or lend a helping paw at a **MEWLLION** dollar fundraiser. Len is one classy kitty; his suit is never wrinkled, and his bowtie is never crooked. The only son of a fashion **MEOWDEL** and a technological **ENTRE-PAW-NEUR**, Len knows that money purrs and he's got enough milk in his fridge to prove it.

LIKES: MEWGO BOSS suits, 2% milk—shaken, not stirred
DISLIKES: Sweatpants
FAVORITE SNACK: Caviar
HOBBIES: Managing companies, making deals
FAVORITE TOY: Mouse-shaped piggy bank
MOTTO: "Money can't buy happiness, but it can buy milkz!"
LIFE DREAM: To trade on the MEW YORK Stock Exchange

MEET Tightz!

Tightz is an ex-circus kitty with a **SAR-CAT-STIC** streak. No kitty is sure if his stilt-like legs are real or just leftover props from the **BARNUM & TAILEY** Circus, but he walks on them as if they're just regular paws. Tightz might be a retired performer, but he still likes to flex his **ACRO-CAT** skills every now and then. He can leap from the TV onto the ceiling fan and spin around and around before landing with a flourish! But if he's not practicing his feats of flight, you'll find him on the couch making sassy remarks. Me-oww!

LIKES: Soaring through the air
DISLIKES: Poorly built ceiling fans
FAVORITE SNACK: Kettle corn
HOBBIES: Listening to PAWD-CASTS, practicing flips
FAVORITE TOY: Orange cat tree with extra-high platforms
MOTTO: "Not my circus. Not my kitties."
LIFE DREAM: To perfect an ACRO-CAT'S most difficult trick: The Upside-Down Mousemaker

WORKINIT
SERIES 2

Bonez's rap career began with freestyles rapped directly to his...mirror. But even though he started out with stage fright, he now **PAW-FORMS** in twenty shows a month, swagging through a different city every week. When Bonez hits the stage, his fans become **HISS-TERICAL**! He's so **PAW-PULAR** that he gets crates of milk sent to his dressing room before every show. Bonez's lyrics really hit home to a lot of kitties; he raps about trying to survive on tuna scraps, and dodging fake **FURRIENDS**. His beats are so boss, even dogs like him!

LIKES: Dope beats, loud crowds
DISLIKES: PAW-PARAZZI
FAVORITE SNACK: M&Ms
HOBBIES: Writing lyrics, PAW-FORMING, giving back to the CLAWMMUNITY
FAVORITE TOY: Fish bone chain
MOTTO: "I've got 99 problems, but a mouse ain't one!"
LIFE DREAM: To have 10 albums go platinum

ITTY BITTY KITTIES

MY PAWZ ARE SMOL BUT MY HEART IS BIG!

MEET
Baby Bucketz!

#ALLGROWEDUP

That's *Lady* Baby Bucketz to you! The smallest kitty in Her **MEOWJESTY'S ORDER OF THE PAW**, Baby Bucketz takes her duties very seriously. Okay no, nobody knows she's a knight, and no, she hasn't been called to go on any missions yet, but she spends a few hours a day practicing her sword fighting and **MEOWSTING** (although she hasn't found a horse to ride, so it's mostly her running into the wall with a lance in her paw). Rarely seen without her little bucket helmet, teeny Baby Bucketz never backs down, never surrenders, and only stops her daily practice for snack time!

LIKES: Fighting for all that is good
DISLIKES: Bedtime
FAVORITE SNACK: Chocolate milk
HOBBIES: Challenging kitties to duels, being gallant
FAVORITE TOY: Her (cardboard) sword, EXCALI-PURR
MOTTO: "I iz ur knight in shining paw-mor."
LIFE DREAM: To own a castle

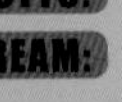

MEET

Arnold!

#ALLGROWEDUP

Nobody tell Arnold his glasses are on upside-down, please. He will be so embarrassed! Teeny Arnold loves to tell the other kitties about facts and figures that he reads about in his books. He can always be seen padding around by stacks and stacks of the heaviest tomes the library has, firmly pushing his giant spectacles up his itty-bitty face. He'll squint at the pages and sniff knowingly, licking his toe beans before turning to the next page. He's so serious about his books that the other kitties don't have the heart to tell him—he's forgotten one little thing: he doesn't know how to read!

LIKES: Books, journals, newspapers
DISLIKES: When books are checked out
FAVORITE SNACK: Peanut butter and jellyfish sandwiches
HOBBIES: Turning pages, lifting heavy books, CAT-EARING his favorite books
FAVORITE TOY: Who needs toys when you have books?
MOTTO: "I'm dah smartest kitteh around!"
LIFE DREAM: To learn how to read

MEET

Karen!

#ALLGROWEDUP

Fur? Fierce. Shoes? Strutting. Paws? Polished. Little Karen is ready to hit the mall. Shopping isn't just a hobby for this boss kitty. Karen's on a first-name basis with manager of **LOUIS KITTEN**, **NEIMAN MEOWCUS**, and **FURBERRY**. When she walks in the store, whiskers start whispering, because she came to spend her **COLLAR BILLS** and you can bet she always makes an entrance. No kitty is sure how itty-bitty Karen manages to pay for all of her fish-flavored lipsticks and designer tail bracelets, but one thing is **FUR** sure: she shops till she drops.

LIKES: Jewelry, credit cards
DISLIKES: Waiting in line
FAVORITE SNACK: Vanilla soy latte with extra milk, no foam
HOBBIES: Shopping, shopping, and, um—hello? Shopping!
FAVORITE TOY: Gold shopping bag
MOTTO: "U work on CAT-MISSION, right? Big mistake. Huge!"
LIFE DREAM: To live in a mansion

MEET Mahhk!

Mahhk has loved baseball his whole life. He was born right on home plate at FUR-NWAY PARK! He knows the stadium like the back of his little paw; he's snacked at the CAT-CESSION stand, been a ball kitty, and even tried to fit into the mascot uniform for the home team! But this kitty has yet to play a minute during a real game. Once, he caught a foul ball that flew into the stands—but he had to give that back. Mahhk isn't worried—he can practically feel himself on that field, listening to the roar of APPAWSE from the crowd. Play ball!

LIKES: Empty baseball parks
DISLIKES: Bad calls
FAVORITE SNACK: Peanuts and/or Cracker Jacks
HOBBIES: Imaginary bunting, imaginary throwing, imaginary sliding into home plate
FAVORITE TOY: His cat scratcher shaped like a baseball bat
MOTTO: "Did I getz a home run?"
LIFE DREAM: To pitch at FUR-NWAY Park during a real game

MEET Jordan!

Jordan comes from a family of cobblers—shoemakers with speed and style that's unmatched! Their designs are in high demand in the FUR-SHION industry and in the world of CATHLETICS, but there's just one problem. Little Jordan is supposed to inherit the shoe empire someday, but his footwork isn't fancy enough to keep up! Jordan's teeny paws are helpless at sewing. The only thing Jordan has ever been good at is CAT-SKETBALL, but he hasn't quite PURRED up the courage to tell his parents that when he grows up, he wants to leave the fast-paced world of shoemaking behind to be PAW-FESSIONAL CATHLETE.

LIKES: Dribbling the CAT-SKETBALL
DISLIKES: Heels, sandals, loafers
FAVORITE SNACK: Treaties, the catnip-flavored cereal
HOBBIES: Shooting FUR THROWS, practicing his dunk
FAVORITE TOY: His first pair of CATHLETIC shoes
MOTTO: "I haz big shoez to fill."
LIFE DREAM: To be drafted in the NCA (National CAT-SKETBALL League) with the big kitties

MEET
Miss Chievous!

#ALLGROWEDUP

Miss Chievous has her beauty routine down to a science. First, she puts on foundation to make sure her fur is the **PURR-FECT** shade of yellow. Next, she makes sure to do her cat contour—how else will other kitties know she looks this good from every angle? Then comes lip-gloss, which is tuna flavored and usually ends up all over her face and not just her mouth. Oops! But hey, **THE MORE THE HAIRIER** when it comes to beauty, right? Last, teeny Miss Chievous puts on her eye shadow in the most **PAW-SOME** purple color. Meow wow—so natural.

LIKES: Highlighter, blush, PAW-FUME
DISLIKES: Messing up her winged eyeliner
FAVORITE SNACK: Tuna-flavored lip-gloss
HOBBIES: Watching beauty tutorials online
FAVORITE TOY: Pink paw mirror
MOTTO: "Dis face iz fierce!"
LIFE DREAM: To start her own MEWTUBE beauty channel

MEET
Happy Pants!

Poor little Happy Pants has had it up to HERE with the kitties at his school. On school picture day last year their prank went off early, so the sound of a dog barking blasted just as his photo was taken. He jumped so high that all you could see in the picture was the tip of his tail! This year, they dipped his favorite tie in milk, thinking it belonged to their principal. Happy Pants hates pranks, but he knows that when he grows up, he's going to become a teacher, and then **HE'LL MAKE THE RULES**.

LIKES: Ties, cravats, justice
DISLIKES: Pranks
FAVORITE SNACK: Black coffee (decaffeinated)
HOBBIES: Making sure no one steals from the Lost and Found, checking hall passes
FAVORITE TOY: His fish-shaped lunchbox
MOTTO: "Say no thankz to prankz!"
LIFE DREAM: To have summer vacation all year long

#ALLPLAY

TO-DO LIST 4 THE DAY: PLAY, PLAY, PLAY, PLAY!

MEET

Danger McGee!

#ALLPLAY

Look, up in the sky! What do you see? It's a bird, it's a plane, it's...DANGER MCGEE! When you're training to be a stunt kitty, you've got to be **TOUGH AS TUNA**, but little Danger McGee has what it takes. When he isn't crashing through glass doors or pretending to be on fire, Danger McGee is screeching out of the sky to surprise unsuspecting kitties, always landing in a daring pose. If it doesn't at least have the *possibility* of giving him a scar, Danger McGee doesn't see the point. This tiny kitty is **FUR-OCIOUS, IM-PURRVIOUS** to pain, and not afraid of anything (except the milk running out).

LIKES: Danger

DISLIKES: Being interrupted mid-stunt

FAVORITE SNACK: Catnip granola bar (for the quick energy boost)

HOBBIES: Skydiving, crashing, tumbling, kicking the air

FAVORITE TOY: Yellow wand toy

MOTTO: "Danger iz mah middle name. Actually, iz my first name. I IZ EVEN MORE DANGEROUS."

LIFE DREAM: To become a famous Hollywood stunt kitty and star in action MEW-VIES

MEET

Steve!

Online, little Steve is an itty bit intimidating. After MEOWSTERING the PAWSTATION 4, he went on to win dozens of gaming competitions. What no kitty knows is that Steve's so good at gaming because he just loves pushing buttons. He couldn't tell you what half of those buttons even do! But when his little paws land on the controller, they go into hyper-speed, and—before you know it—his OP-PAW-NENT has tasted the bitter milk of defeat. GAME OVER.

LIKES: Twelve-button controllers
DISLIKES: Touch-screens
FAVORITE SNACK: Gumdrop buttons
HOBBIES: Playing Whack-a-Mouse and Hungry Hungry Hippos
FAVORITE TOY: Controller with the big, red button
MOTTO: "Don't push urself. Push buttonz!"
LIFE DREAM: To become AMBI-CAT-STROUS and push buttons just as fast using all four paws

MEET

Beebles!

There's nothing Beebles loves more than bugs. Walking outside with Beebles is like being in a whole different MEW-NIVERSE. She gasps at the sight of a bumblebee, giggles at dragonflies, and delights in the smell that a stinkbug leaves behind. Bitty Beebles always gets lost in what she's doing. Paws deep in the dirt and nose in the grass, she watches bugs with the same excitement she gets from running her claws down a scratching post. But this sweet kitty wouldn't hurt a fly (literally)!

LIKES: The titan beetle, the common bumblebee, the red-fanged funnel spider
DISLIKES: Lawn mowers and other bug-killers
FAVORITE SNACK: Farm-fresh catnip
HOBBIES: Looking at bugs, wondering about bugs
FAVORITE TOY: Her shiny specimen jar
MOTTO: "One little bee makez such a big difference. Why can't one little Beebles?"
LIFE DREAM: To discover a new species of bug

MEET
DJ 9-Lives!

If a **PAW-TY** is rocking, you'd best believe that DJ 9-Lives is the one rocking it. This kitty's headphones might be the size of his entire body, but you can bet his beats are big! When DJ 9-Lives scratches the discs, the tails start thumping, the whiskers start waving, and paws go up in the air like they just don't care! Hold onto your catnip, because when the bass drops, it's going to change all nine of your lives. DJ 9-Lives always knows the right song to set the mood, and there's always one mood to set: **FUN**!

LIKES: Sound effects
DISLIKES: Equipment malfunctions
FAVORITE SNACK: Candied beets
HOBBIES: DJ'ing CAT-MITZVAHS, dancing to the MEOWSIC
FAVORITE TOY: His digital turntables
MOTTO: "Allz I do iz spin, spin, spin no matter what!"
LIFE DREAM: To be a world-famous DJ

MEET
Cici Queen!

Cici Queen is the happiest kitty on four paws, but she only plays the blues. Sweet tunes from her trumpet never fail to make grown kitties cry. Cici Queen doesn't say much—but her trumpet tootles out the teeny tunes when the words won't come. No kitty has seen her without her trumpet clutched in her paws at all times. Cici Queen's playing is as smooth as salmon mousse on a Sunday, and you can catch her at the Cat Café every weekend, **MAKING HER TRUMPET PURR**.

LIKES: Learning new meowsic
DISLIKES: Being out of tune (or out of tuna)
FAVORITE SNACK: Catfish
HOBBIES: Paw-forming, practicing, cleaning her trumpet
FAVORITE TOY: Catnip ladybug
MOTTO: "When wordz fail, meowisc speakz."
LIFE DREAM: To learn to play another horn

MEET
Slopez!

#ALLPLAY

Slopez is ready to shred the *fresh pow*. Ready to make *first tracks* on the mountain. Ready to *tear it up*. Okay, okay—so Slopez isn't what you'd call an expert sledder. She has the sled, she has the gear, but when she gets ready to cruise, her paws just don't do what she tells them! Whiskers frozen, eyes shut, yowling for all she's worth, little Slopez spends the majority of her mountain adventures as a total SCAREDY-CAT. But even though her tail trembles (and not from the cold), she always climbs back up the mountain for round two. Now *that's* gnarly!

LIKES: Freshly fallen snow
DISLIKES: Landing whiskers-deep in freshly fallen snow
FAVORITE SNACK: Hot cocoa with MARSHMEOWS
HOBBIES: Falling, screaming, making snow kitties
FAVORITE TOY: Her cozy hat
MOTTO: "Iz I at the bottom of dah hill yet? I can't look!"
LIFE DREAM: To MEOWSTER a black diamond run

MEET
Trixie!

#ALLPLAY

Tiny Trixie is just that—tricky. She is the first kitty ever to win a **THREE-PAWED** race all by herself, she set the record win for the egg-on-spoon race after finishing in less than four seconds, and even has a plaque hanging in a restaurant in **MEOWCHESTER**, England, where she won the World's Largest Pie-Eating Contest three years in a row. Little Trixie is good at a lot of things (sixty-seven and counting), but she's best at the hula-hoop. She'll wake up with her trusty hoop already around her hips, and do the hula through breakfast, lunch, and dinner! One kitty swears that Trixie takes the hula-hoop to the bathroom with her, but that can't be true...can it?

LIKES: Competing
DISLIKES: Getting second place
FAVORITE SNACK: Fruit Loopz
HOBBIES: Hula-hooping, trying new things
FAVORITE TOY: Twisty red hula-hoop (her lucky color!)
MOTTO: "Oh, iz I the winner? Again?"
LIFE DREAM: To own 100 trophies

MEET

Yawnz!

No, no, no do NOT turn off the TV: Yawnz is watching that. It may look like this kitty's eyes are closed, but she's just getting all of her blinks out now in case she's in an extra-intense staring contest later. Anyway, she is SO not even sleepy; it's just that the room is warm like freshly toasted **MARSHMEOWS** and this blanket feel so soft on her little paws, and the music coming from the next room is so soothing. See? **PURR-LY** circumstantial. She is NOT tired. Huh uh, no way.

LIKES: Late nights
DISLIKES: When kitties tell her that she snores
FAVORITE SNACK: Peanut butter cookies
HOBBIES: Watching MEW-VIES, listening to slow music, resting her eyes
FAVORITE TOY: Her stuffed octopus, Glen
MOTTO: "Zzzzzzzzzzz."
LIFE DREAM: To be the host of a late night show

MEET

Tike!

CUTIEPAWTOOTIE

Tike wants candy *always*, and Tike *always* gets what he wants! The littlest kitty from a litter of ten, Tike used to be pushed around nonstop. But one day he realized that his little body and big eyes are **PAW-FECT** for getting kitties to hand over their candy at the drop of a purr. Now the world is his candy store, and he's got sticky little paws. Tike's not used to hearing "no," but when he does, it's nothing that a bit of eyelash fluttering can't fix. It's like taking candy from a kitten!

LIKES: Candy canes, candy coins, candy corn
DISLIKES: Bullies
FAVORITE SNACK: All 49 flavors of jellybeans in one big ball
HOBBIES: Giving the KITTY-CAT eyes
FAVORITE TOY: Plastic peppermint stick
MOTTO: "Hello, iz the candy police. Give me ur candy."
LIFE DREAM: To open a candy shop

MEET
Buzzy!

#CUTIEPAWTOOTIE

A humming sound breaks the silence of an empty room. It strikes fear into the hearts of mice and kitties alike. It grows louder and louder until—POUNCE! Itty bitty Buzzy strikes, wrangling yarn balls and catnip fish like the MEOWSTER hunter she is. All kitties shudder at the sight of her pink fur standing on end! Okay, so she could be more intimidating. And a little stealthier. That humming sound is her danger music, and she can't help but sing it under her breath when she's getting ready for an ambush. Maybe that's how the last twelve birds have gotten away...

LIKES: Action MEW-VIES
DISLIKES: Kitties who pretend to not be afraid of her
FAVORITE SNACK: Bagel bites
HOBBIES: Stalking, sneaking, attacking
FAVORITE TOY: Wind-up mouse
MOTTO: "I iz pouncing off dah wallz."
LIFE DREAM: To catch a rare bird (or any bird—any bird will do)

MEET
Archie Pawz!

Archie Pawz isn't short. He is vertically challenged. This little kitty is always reaching for the trees, but heights aren't exactly his FUR-TÉ. Archie Pawz wants to be up there with the big kitties! He wants to fly in airplanes fifty-thousand feet in the air! He wants to lean over the edge of skyscrapers and look down at the city below! He wants to be able to reach the cabinet above the fridge where the kitties hid the catnip! Poor Archie is just a little guy with fridge-sized ambition, but one day he's going to get his paws all the way to the top.

#CUTIEPAWTOOTIE

LIKES: Growing
DISLIKES: Height limits on roller coasters
FAVORITE SNACK: Milk Duds, heavy on the milk
HOBBIES: Stretching to encourage paw growth, using other kitties as stepping stools to climb higher
FAVORITE TOY: Multicolored feather toy
MOTTO: "U can measure ur height, but not ur heart!"
LIFE DREAM: To grow taller by two tail lengths!

MEET

McGiggle z!

#CUTIEPAWTOOTIE

Little McGigglez loves to laugh. And nothing gets her giggle going better than the mail! But when McGigglez laughs, her little paws turn to little claws, and the mail gets a little bit...shredded. Bills, cut into ribbons. Magazines, diced like tomatoes. And her **FUR-VORITE**; coupons sliced to smithereens. The mail never gets further than the front door on days where mini McGigglez is manning the mail slot, but no kitty can get mad at her. I mean—look at that cutie-cat's face!

LIKES: Manila envelopes, international stamps
DISLIKES: P.O. boxes
FAVORITE SNACK: Alphabet soup
HOBBIES: Laughing, giggling, chuckling
FAVORITE TOY: Clown kitten squeaker toy
MOTTO: "I Iz the mail monster. Hear me giggle."
LIFE DREAM: To break into the POST PAW-FFICE and just go wild

MEET

Bubz Jr.!

#CUTIEPAWTOOTIE

Bubz Jr. is the teeniest of kitties with the biggest dreams. He once went to a magic show where he saw a famous bubble artist blowing beautiful shaped bubbles. Butterflies, balls of yarn, TUNA! You name it, he could make a bubble of it. Bubz Jr. loves bubbles, but he loves it more when they POP! So he padded out into the ring and pop, pop, popped until his little prickly paws could pop no more! The bubble artist and the crowd were shocked, but Bubz Jr. was just being his bubbly self. What's a kitty to do?

LIKES: Organic bubble mixture
DISLIKES: Hard-to-reach bubbles that float away from him
FAVORITE SNACK: Bubble gum
HOBBIES: Blowing bubbles, popping the bubbles
FAVORITE TOY: Yellow bubble wand passed down from Bubz Sr.
MOTTO: "Keep ur kittehs close and ur bubbles closer!"
LIFE DREAM: To pop a bubble the size of a BUS

#HOMEBODIEZ

SORRY I CAN'T, I HAZ TO DO NOTHING!

MEET

Snagglez!

#HOMEBODIEZ

Snagglez's fur has a mind of its own. Some kitties have said it even changes color with his moods. Snagglez brushes it every day, but it's so thick that he keeps finding surprises stuck inside. He's found a sock back there, several old fur brushes, a family of ladybugs, and the caps of seven pens (only the caps). Not only is his fur a little bit tangled, but little Snagglez has a crooked smile, too. One tooth likes to break free from the pack and poke out of his mouth. But Snagglez knows that his smile is nothing short of **SNAGGLE-FABULOUS**.

LIKES: Deep-conditioning shampoo, prescription toothpaste

DISLIKES: Losing his keys in his fur

FAVORITE SNACK: Raspberry-flavored fur gel

HOBBIES: Brushing his fur, posing in all reflective surfaces, playing checkers

FAVORITE TOY: His trusty red fur brush, HAIRY STYLEZ

MOTTO: "Snaggle hair, don't care!"

LIFE DREAM: To become a magazine MEOWDEL

MEET Vomz!

Poor little Vomz is always coming down with something, whether it's IN-FUR-ENZA, KITTEN POX, or a super strong strain of HISSING COUGH. He once missed singing the solo in a recital because he was stuck in bed with a bad case of BRON-CAT-IS. Vomz is a teeny bad luck machine, and if there's an illness that a kitty can get, you can bet that he's already had it—twice. Vomz hates missing out, so his room is almost all windows, that way he can supervise the other kitties' fun, even if he can't always PURR-TICIPATE.

LIKES: Milk-flavored cough medicine
DISLIKES: Phlegm, mucus, headaches, tail aches
FAVORITE SNACK: Fish-shaped vitamins
HOBBIES: Making blanket forts, checking his temperature
FAVORITE TOY: Light blue hypoallergenic pillow
MOTTO: "U get better or u get bitter. Or u get butter. Peanut butter."
LIFE DREAM: To go a whole year without being sick

MEET Lil' Miss!

Hug **PAW-TY**, coming through! Lil' Miss is hugs-over-hisses, every time. She is the self-appointed conflict resolution kitty that can solve even the most **HAIR-RAISING** catfights. Something about Lil' Miss's calm **CATTITUDE** and outstretched paws makes every kitty stop in the middle of a hissy fit—she has the **MEOWGIC** touch! Lovely Lil' Miss even holds workshops for kitties who need a little hugging help, with team-building exercises and **MICE CREAM SOCIALS** at the end!

LIKES: Making new friends, ten-minute hugs
DISLIKES: Kitties who lie and say they don't like hugs
FAVORITE SNACK: Candy hearts
HOBBIES: Hugging, squeezing, teaching the art of hugging and squeezing
FAVORITE TOY: Her purple stuffed kitty Lady Snugglebottom
MOTTO: "A hugz gotta use both paws. Bring it in."
LIFE DREAM: To teach troubled kitties the power of hugs

MEET
Poofles!

What time is bath time? ALL THE TIME! At least it is in the land of the Great Empress of Bubbles: Little Lady Poofles! Sitting on her throne (tub) she gives orders to her subjects (bubbles) and has the most fun a kitty can have with just a little soap and water! She makes bubble beards, bubble wands, bubble MER-KITTY tails so she can delve into bubble kingdoms under the deep blue... bathtub! It might seem like Poofles sticks to her tub most of the time, but this kitty is always floating on her imaginary bubbles to new worlds.

LIKES: Catnip-scented bubble bath
DISLIKES: Cold bathwater
FAVORITE SNACK: Dippin' Dots mice cream
HOBBIES: Conquering bubble cities, riding on bubble horses, defeating bubble monsters
FAVORITE TOY: Her trusty orange tub
MOTTO: "All u need iz fish, hope, and bubble soap!"
LIFE DREAM: To have a bathtub so big she can swim in it

MEET
Crinkleplum!

Cutie-pie Crinkleplum is always crackling with excitement. Literally. The king of static cling has a coat that's always one paw touch away from a ZAP, thanks to his love of the dryer. When a kitty's clothes go missing, Crinkleplum the laundry fiend is the one to blame. He just loves burying himself in a basket fresh from the machine, so he snatches clothes up just so he can toss them in the dryer—clean or dirty, it doesn't matter to him! And Crinkleplum's favorite place to go is nowhere, so he has all the time in the world for a relaxing basket bath. PURR-FECT!

LIKES: The smell of dryer sheets, fluffy towels
DISLIKES: Empty hampers
FAVORITE SNACK: Plums
HOBBIES: Snuggling, shocking, stealing
FAVORITE TOY: Empty bottle of fabric softener
MOTTO: "Snap, crinkle, PLUM!"
LIFE DREAM: To build a cat cave made entirely of dryer sheets

#NOMZ

SNACK TIME IZ MY FAV TIME!

MEET Paddles!

#NOMZ

Tiny Paddles operates under a strict lick-and-leave policy. She spots your food, licks it, and then **HIGH-TAILS** it out of there on **PADDLING** paws, lickety-split! This mischievous kitty is eager for a bite of just about everything, whether it belongs to her or not. She learned to lick-and-leave after finishing an entire batch of cookie dough all by herself and being greeted by one angry baker. Apparently, kitties don't like her legendary licking? How weird! So now Paddles sticks to quick slurps and leaves before the drool is dry.

LIKES: Garnishes, frostings, sauces

DISLIKES: When kitties finish their food before *she* can

FAVORITE SNACK: Licking just the chocolate off of chocolate-covered raisins

HOBBIES: Drooling, licking, slurping

FAVORITE TOY: Waterproof laser pointer

MOTTO: "Lick first, ask questionz later."

LIFE DREAM: To lick each of the Seven Wonders of the World

MEET

Cheekz!

#NOMZ

Cutie-pie Cheekz is not interested in **PAW-TION** control. She wants more, more, more and she wants it **RIGHT MEOW**! This means that sometimes she isn't the most careful eater—once she had a double helping of what turned out to be wall insulation before she realized it wasn't cotton candy. And, to be fair, it did have a sweet blue flavor, so all in all, not the worst snack she's ever had! This teeny kitten can store up to fifty snacks at a time in the pouches of her cheeks, and despite her somewhat sturdy body, you can usually find her in a tree up to fifty feet off the ground!

LIKES: Seconds, thirds
DISLIKES: Diets
FAVORITE SNACK: Whatever you've got! What's that? In your hand? GIVE ME THAT.
HOBBIES: Lining her cheeks with steak sauce (yum)
FAVORITE TOY: Catnip acorn
MOTTO: "May the fork be with u."
LIFE DREAM: To grow a tail pouch and keep extra snacks inside

MEET

Meatball!

#NOMZ

Did some kitty say...PASTA?! Meatball is crazy for carbs, loony for noodles, totally bonkers for bucatini! Other kitties have learned that when he's had his ninth bowl of fettuccine alfredo, it's best to stay out of his way or get caught in the rigatoni rampage. Little Meatball once climbed all the way to the roof of a local Italian restaurant and had eaten his way through four of their plaster meatballs before someone called the **FIRE DE-PAWTMENT** and got him down. Meatball isn't a dangerous kitty, he's just a hungry one...or at least that's what he says when he wakes up somewhere, covered in sauce. No regrets.

LIKES: Lasagna, linguine, tortellini, cannelloni
DISLIKES: Al dente noodles
FAVORITE SNACK: A big bowl of spaghetti and meatballs

HOBBIES: Eating pasta, making pasta
FAVORITE TOY: Blue spaghetti bowl
MOTTO: "Pasta la vista, kitteh!"
LIFE DREAM: To move to Italy

MEET
Butternut!

Itty bitty Butternut has butterpaws. He can't hold onto anything! MICE CREAM? PLOP. Freshly baked soufflé? Forget about it. Newborn kitten? Oops. Don't worry, even kittens land on their feet...right? Butternut can't help it—he's always been this way. This teeny kitty once tried catching a football on the field, and, well...he doesn't want to get into the whole story...but let's just say the school ended up completely destroyed. Despite his problem paws, Butternut still grabs at every slippery food in sight. He's accepted that in life it's NOMZ OR NOTHING!

LIKES: Mice cream, banana peels, applesauce
DISLIKES: Dropping food
FAVORITE SNACK: Pureed piranha
HOBBIES: Eating, falling, football (he hasn't been kicked out of every league yet)
FAVORITE TOY: Green bouncy ball
MOTTO: "Every part of me iz clumsy but my tummy!"
LIFE DREAM: To puree his own piranha without letting the fish escape (again)

MEET
Marvin!

NOMZ

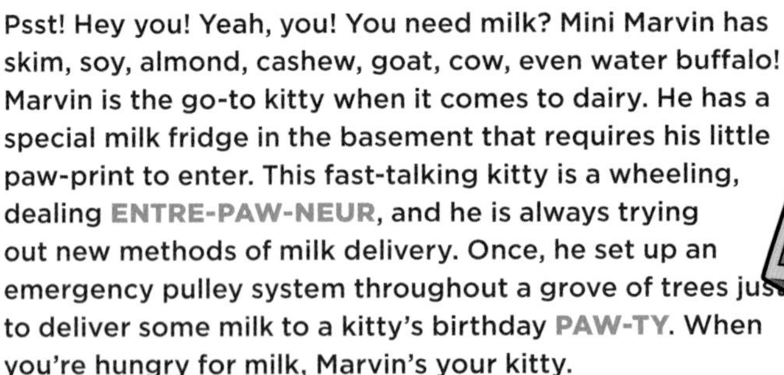

Psst! Hey you! Yeah, you! You need milk? Mini Marvin has skim, soy, almond, cashew, goat, cow, even water buffalo! Marvin is the go-to kitty when it comes to dairy. He has a special milk fridge in the basement that requires his little paw-print to enter. This fast-talking kitty is a wheeling, dealing ENTRE-PAW-NEUR, and he is always trying out new methods of milk delivery. Once, he set up an emergency pulley system throughout a grove of trees just to deliver some milk to a kitty's birthday PAW-TY. When you're hungry for milk, Marvin's your kitty.

LIKES: Money, milk, milk money
DISLIKES: Competitors
FAVORITE SNACK: Chilled milk in a martini glass, no ice
HOBBIES: Networking, getting down to business
FAVORITE TOY: Gold milk carton (it was a gift from a client)
MOTTO: "Milk iz money."
LIFE DREAM: To own a dairy farm so he can be his own supplier

MEET
Piccato!

#UGHOHZ

Once puny Piccato starts painting, he just can't stop! Sometimes he even uses his itty-bitty tail instead of his brush to paint those hard-to-reach spots. And for Piccato, THE WORLD IS HIS CANVAS. Couches, carpet, walls inside houses, walls outside houses, sidewalks, nearby trees, once even a little mouse that scurried across his path. Piccato can't help it—when the urge to paint hits him, he has to put his paws to work or risk losing his MEWS! Unfortunately, it's hard to explain inspiration when other kitties noticed you've tracked painted paw-prints all over their catnip. Oops!

LIKES: Watercolor, oil paints
DISLIKES: Accidentally drinking from the mug of white paint instead of milk
FAVORITE SNACK: Artichoke dip
HOBBIES: Painting, sketching, drawing
FAVORITE TOY: Lucky paintbrush with the long handle
MOTTO: "Painting iz like purring wiff color."
LIFE DREAM: To create a MEOWSTERPIECE that will hang in a famous gallery

MEET
T. P. Rollerton!

It's not T. P. Rollerton's fault! The toilet paper started it! The toilet paper *always* starts it. Teeny T. P. Rollerton likes to visit the bathroom to eat her daily snack—it's not weird! But then the toilet paper looks at her with those two-ply eyes and something about the roll just whispers in her ear, "What if you unrolled me? All of me?" Before she knows it, she's wrapped up in toilet paper like the spookiest mummy kitty on Halloween, buried under piles of quilted double-soft, with floating bits falling like snow all over the bathroom.

LIKES: Extra-thick toilet paper
DISLIKES: Having to clean up her mess
FAVORITE SNACK: Candy wrappers
HOBBIES: Making toilet paper forts, munching on empty toilet paper rolls
FAVORITE TOY: Ball of twine
MOTTO: "U just gotta ROLL WIFF IT."
LIFE DREAM: To finally defeat her nemesis: the toilet paper

UGHOHZ

There's nothing that itty-bitty Burt likes better than DIRT! He's most at home when he's in a three-foot hole, covered in soil, greeting the roots and flowers with a morning song. Burt has a GREEN PAW, and growing things have a tendency to sprout up around him (and even *in* his fur sometimes). This kitty is fascinated by anything floral, and you'll often find him whiskers-deep in the dirt, purring over the petals of a peony. But Burt's not great with boundaries—he's been known to pot his plants RIGHT in the milk, leave seeds sprouting in the catnip, and track little muddy pawprints all over the floor.

LIKES: VENUS FUR TRAPS, PURR-ANIUMS

DISLIKES: Dry weather

FAVORITE SNACK: Honeysuckle flowers

HOBBIES: Planting, watering, whispering to the plants

FAVORITE TOY: Little red bucket with the leaky sides

MOTTO: "Why iz u going when u could be growing?"

LIFE DREAM: To grow a house out of flowers and live in it, covered in mud

MEET Sheldon!

All hail Sheldon, the Sultan of Slime! Wondering what that greenish-yellowish thing is hanging from the ceiling, the backs of chairs, on those paintings, all through the neighborhood, and swinging from trees? That is the work of a MEOWSTER, and little Sheldon takes full credit. Well...sometimes. Sometimes the other kitties think his MEOWSTERPIECES of slime art are smelly and gross and messy. Messy! Are you KITTEN me? So Sheldon gives them his cutest, most innocent look to throw them off his tail. Huh? What do you mean his teeny paws are covered in green goop?

LIKES: Glow-in-the-dark slime

DISLIKES: Art critics

FAVORITE SNACK: Seaweed wraps

HOBBIES: PAW-VANTE GARDE slime painting

FAVORITE TOY: Wavy cardboard scratcher

MOTTO: "Slime healz all woundz."

LIFE DREAM: To craft his own brand of extra-smelly slime covered in sparkles

MEET
Hugger!

#UGHOHZ

Huggable Hugger loves everyone and everything—maybe a little too much. See, Hugger is strong for such a small kitty, with more power in his little paws than he knows what to do with. In school he gets mistaken for a grown-up kitty so often that he sometimes sneaks into the teacher's lounge and snatches snacks for the other itty bitty kitties. Hugger loves making friends, but his friends have a little trouble with his hugs. He just hangs on a *little* too tight. Clingy Hugger is a well-meaning kitty—he just has attachment issues. As in, if he loves something, he will **NEVER LET IT GO**.

LIKES: Squeezing with all of his might
DISLIKES: Accidentally making his friends pass out from "lack of oxygen"
FAVORITE SNACK: Squeezy cheese
HOBBIES: Hugging, tackling, wrestling, cat piles
FAVORITE TOY: Balloons!
MOTTO: "Nobody'z bugged if everybody'z hugged!"
LIFE DREAM: To have his friends follow the hug schedule he prints out for them every day

MEET
Violet Pots!

#UGHOHZ

Dainty little Violet Pots is the prettiest flower you'll ever see—and not just because she's eaten the rest of the flowers and planted herself in a pot. She can't help it—**CAT-SANTHYMUMS**, **DAFF-FUR-DILS**, **AMARYLL-HISS**? They're all so lovely...and delicious. Nothing tastes better to this kitty than petals, and nothing feels better than dirt between her **TOE BEANS**. Rumor has it that Violet Pots used to be a **NEAT FUR-REAK**—she needed to have everything spic-and-span, and she hardly ever left the house. Now, nothing can hold her back! Except Burt if he catches her eating his **PURR-ANIUMS**. Whoops—were those yours?

LIKES: Springtime
DISLIKES: Pesticides
FAVORITE SNACK: Buttercup smoothie
HOBBIES: Enjoying the flora, eating the flora
FAVORITE TOY: Clay pot (it's just her size!)
MOTTO: "Sometimez u just gotta stop and EAT THE ROSES."
LIFE DREAM: To taste every flower flavor in the garden

KIT-TWINS

MEET Beanz & Grumblez!

The only time Beanz and Grumblez aren't arguing is when they're eating, and that's only because it's not **PAW-LITE** to yowl with your mouth full! Beanz and Grumblez scheme for meals and swipe snacks whenever they get the chance. Beanz has the gift of glide—she can be in and out of a room so quickly, it's like she didn't even lift a paw! Grumblez is the distraction—one loud burp from Grumblez and the coast is clear, the city is clear—the whole country is clear. But even though they're a team, Beanz and Grumblez will still throw down over even the *tiniest* bit of tuna.

BEANZ

LIKES: Roller skating
DISLIKES: When Grumblez beats her to the bowl
FAVORITE SNACK: Extra-large slushy
HOBBIES: Looting, sliding, snatching
FAVORITE TOY: Empty can of beans that rattles
MOTTO: "Eat what u can! Givez nothing back."
LIFE DREAM: To have her own slushy machine

GRUMBLEZ

LIKES: The sweet taste of stolen salmon
DISLIKES: When Beanz hides food from her
FAVORITE SNACK: Microwavable breakfast PURRITOS
HOBBIES: Burping, belching, grabbing
FAVORITE TOY: Plastic fish with the broken squeaker
MOTTO: "Sharing iz caring. Unless it'z my foodz."
LIFE DREAM: To clean out an entire grocery store

MEET Poser & Peeper!

Poser and Peeper don't always see eye to eye. Poser is an aspiring **MEOWDEL**, so he's always making sure his fur is on point. His bedroom is less of a place to sleep and more of a 24/7 catwalk. Poser and his mirror are BFF's, and that's Peeper's worst nightmare! Peeper is terrified of mirrors—no one is really sure why. Poser has tried to show Peeper the power of a good pose, but Peeper still walks around the house with her paws over her eyes—just in case!

POSER

LIKES: Himself, in the mirror. So fierce!
DISLIKES: Bad fur days
FAVORITE SNACK: GRANDE MICE COFFEE, extra whipped cream
HOBBIES: Reading magazines, practicing his catwalk, posing
FAVORITE TOY: His IFUR-NE
MOTTO: "2 blessed 2 be stressed."
LIFE DREAM: To be the next Cover Cat

PEEPER

LIKES: Blue skies
DISLIKES: Mirrors
FAVORITE SNACK: Hummus
HOBBIES: Peeping, shrieking, hiding
FAVORITE TOY: Blue ball of yarn
MOTTO: "None of my bizness!"
LIFE DREAM: To live nine drama-free lives

MEET
Hush & Loudmouth!

Brothers by blood and not much else, Hush and Loudmouth are as different as ice-cold milk and tuna fish. Loudmouth has a lot of feelings, and he needs to tell everykitty about them, **RIGHT MEOW**. Hush is the **PAW-PPOSITE**. Sometimes Hush can go so long without a single peep that kitties have put up "MISSING" posters for him, only to notice him on the couch snoozing, having been there all along. Hush tries to be gentle with Loudmouth, so sometimes he *gently* tells Loudmouth to put a sock in it. Quiet!

HUSH

LIKES: Complete and absolute silence
DISLIKES: Motorcycle engines, roosters, air horns
FAVORITE SNACK: Hushpuppies
HOBBIES: Reflecting, deep breathing
FAVORITE TOY: Cloth mouse
MOTTO: "It'z time to be quiet. It'z alwayz time to be quiet."
LIFE DREAM: To live on a quiet, isolated mountaintop

LOUDMOUTH

LIKES: Talking, chatting, yapping
DISLIKES: Complete and absolute silence
FAVORITE SNACK: Cap'n Crunch cereal
HOBBIES: Shouting, yelping, shrieking
FAVORITE TOY: Giant rubber chicken squeaky toy
MOTTO: "Iz all about dah SHOUT!"
LIFE DREAM: To have his own talk show

MEET Pulley & Pullz!

Pulley and Pullz are the dream team. Best friends since the second grade, these two put the "**FUR**" in "**EF-FURT**!" They always give two hundred **PAW-CENT** to every task, and they never **FUR-RENDER.** The problem is, all that **EF-FURT** means that they're both very competitive, and their favorite thing to do is play tug-of-war! What starts as a friendly game turns into a battle of wills, with both kitties pulling on the rope until their paws are sore. They've missed birthday parties, holidays, and work, all for the sake of that sweet tug-of-war. Ready? PULL!

PULLEY

LIKES: Tug-of-war
DISLIKES: Quitting
FAVORITE SNACK: FRUIT BY THE FUR
HOBBIES: Tugging, pulling, yanking
FAVORITE TOY: Rope scratcher
MOTTO: "I iz pulling 4 u."
LIFE DREAM: To finally beat Pullz at tug-of-war (they've always ended in a tie)

PULLZ

LIKES: Tug-of-war
DISLIKES: Losing
FAVORITE SNACK: Grape jelly
HOBBIES: Dragging, stretching, hauling
FAVORITE TOY: Silly putty
MOTTO: "Iz u pulling my paw?"
LIFE DREAM: To finally beat Pulley at tug-of-war (they've always ended in a tie)

MEET Super & Duper!

There is evil in the world, seeking to destroy good kitties and the cat beds they call home. It lurks in the growling of dogs and the roar of thunderstorms. But evil is no match for the **PAW-SOME** kitty powers of Super and Duper! Faster than a speeding **SCAREDY-CAT**, more powerful than fresh catnip, and able to leap tall scratching posts in a single bound—Super is true to her name. Duper is...also there. She can't run very fast, but she always gets there eventually. And she might not be powerful in the *traditional* sense, but she's very good at wordplay. And even though Duper can't leap an entire scratching post, she's skillfully hopped over several cartons of milk in her day. Villains, beware!

SUPER

LIKES: Power-posing, feeling her cape flap in the wind
DISLIKES: Wrongdoing
FAVORITE SNACK: The sweet taste of justice
HOBBIES: Fighting kitty crime, PURR-CHASING replacement capes
FAVORITE TOY: Red eye mask
MOTTO: "I iz the law!"
LIFE DREAM: To scratch out crime FUR good!

DUPER

LIKES: Being invited to the FUR-TRESS of Solitude
DISLIKES: When kitties don't recognize her
FAVORITE SNACK: Pudding
HOBBIES: Giving snappy comebacks, trying to get kitties to guess her secret identity
FAVORITE TOY: Yellow power gloves
MOTTO: "It'z claw-bberin' time!"
LIFE DREAM: To earn a cape of her own

MEET Snoopz & Mr. Liftz!

Okay, here's the plan: using a **PURR-FECTLY** crafted disguise, Snoopz will get on Mr. Liftz's shoulders, and they will **CATWALK** down to the bank. Once inside the bank, the kitty teller will be so in awe of the tall, serious business cat before him that he'll give Snoopz a loan without asking any **HAIRY QUESTIONS**. Once they have the money, it's go time. Snoopz and Mr. Liftz will run to the grocery store dairy aisle and just go nuts. The time for milk is NOW!

SNOOPZ

LIKES: Crazy straws
DISLIKES: Empty milk cartons
FAVORITE SNACK: Double-Bubble gum
HOBBIES: Cooking up schemes with Mr. Liftz, practicing his serious face
FAVORITE TOY: Squeaky fish
MOTTO: "Nuffin 2 see here."
LIFE DREAM: To take a milk bath

MR. LIFTZ

LIKES: Meowsterminding plans
DISLIKES: How short he is
FAVORITE SNACK: Purr-tein powder
HOBBIES: Doing pull-ups, doing push-ups, lifting weights
FAVORITE TOY: Whistling bird toy
MOTTO: "I iz very very tall. I iz a giant."
LIFE DREAM: To drink his weight in milk

MEET Tipz & Upz!

Paw-to-paw, around the tail, through the whiskers, and WHAM! They shoot, they score! Every time. Tipz and Upz are as **CATHLETIC** as can be—name a sport, any sport, and they've **MEOWSTERED** it. Yarn ball? Check. Tennis? Easy. Soccer? They totally kick tail. There's just one problem: Tipz and Upz are incredibly competitive. So competitive that if they're not on the same team, the game just doesn't end! They'll stay out on the field until the stars come out without even breaking a sweat. And whatever Tipz can do, Upz can do too. They are game, set, *matched*!

TIPZ

LIKES: Slam dunks
DISLIKES: REF-FUR-EES
FAVORITE SNACK: CATORADE
HOBBIES: Dribbling, shooting, scoring
FAVORITE TOY: Lucky pink yarn ball
MOTTO: "Swish! Swish! These pawz can't miss."
LIFE DREAM: To play on a PAW-FESSIONAL sports team with Upz

UPZ

LIKES: Home runs
DISLIKES: Foul balls
FAVORITE SNACK: Paw-tein bars
HOBBIES: Hitting, catching, running
FAVORITE TOY: Ball cap with the chewed bill
MOTTO: "Who needz practice when ur already purr-fect?"
LIFE DREAM: To play on a PAW-FESSIONAL sports team with Tipz

MEET Kung & Foo!

Kung & Foo are business **PAW-TNERS**, and their business is dance! Kung used to be a **PAW-FESSIONAL** ballerina, pointing his paws and leaping across the stage. Foo is an ex-alley cat that used to dance for tourists. Now, she and Kung have banded together to choreograph movie fight scenes. Kung gives actors the grace that makes the fighting seem skillful, and Foo gives actors the grit that makes them seem real. They've choreographed fight scenes in films like The **MEOWTRIX**, The **FUR-NE ULTIMATUM**, and The **KARATE CAT**.

KUNG

LIKES: Grand jétes
DISLIKES: Too-small pointe shoes
FAVORITE SNACK: Green grapes
HOBBIES: Going to the ballets for ideas, stretching, staying limber
FAVORITE TOY: Polka-dot ribbon
MOTTO: "U gotta dance like no kitty iz watching."
LIFE DREAM: To open a ballet school for up-and-coming dancers

Foo

LIKES: Reality dance shows
DISLIKES: High MEOW-NTINANCE actors
FAVORITE SNACK: Nachos
HOBBIES: Going to see action MEW-VIES for ideas, working out
FAVORITE TOY: The old FUR-TAR case she used to keep tips in
MOTTO: "I feelz dah dance in my pawz!"
LIFE DREAM: To win an award for kitty choreography

MEET
Shrimp & Stepz!

Shrimp is going to get Stepz fired again—he just knows it. Stepz is a good, upstanding KIT-TIZEN. But his little sister Shrimp is a different story. At every place he's ever worked, she's eaten, destroyed, or lost every product they sold. Shrimp doesn't mean to cause PAW-BLEMS for Stepz—she loves her big brother! Usually she leaves him out of her schemes, but he's just so tall and strong, and sometimes she needs a helping paw. But her paws like trouble more than tuna, and it's only a matter of time until things get fishy!

SHRIMP

LIKES: Testing boundaries
DISLIKES: Order
FAVORITE SNACK: Shrimp scampi
HOBBIES: Poking sleeping bears, playing with spray paint, eating everything she sees
FAVORITE TOY: Red and yellow cat dancer
MOTTO: "Trouble iz fun. Oopz!"
LIFE DREAM: To find the Loch Ness Meownster (and prank it!)

STEPZ

LIKES: Steady pay
DISLIKES: Getting fired
FAVORITE SNACK: Cauliflower
HOBBIES: Working, working overtime, working weekends
FAVORITE TOY: Green deck of cards
MOTTO: "Uh oh. Shrimp strikez again!"
LIFE DREAM: To find a job that Shrimp can't wreck

MEET
Brainz & Brawn!

Brainz and Brawn are the next big thing in **PAW-XING**. These two **CATHLETES** have a **HISSING** rivalry, but there's just one tiny problem: Brainz and Brawn are secretly best **FUR-RIENDS**. No one knows that after big fights, Brainz goes over to Brawn's cat condo to unwind with some milk. No one knows that Brainz drove Brawn to the airport for his last fight. They love to **PAW-X**, but love their **FUR-RIENDSHIP** even more. Think the fans would notice if the claws stayed in the gloves for this match?

BRAINZ

LIKES: Reading the MEWSPAPER
DISLIKES: Missing TAIL DAY at the gym
FAVORITE SNACK: Walnuts
HOBBIES: Watching his old fights on video to learn from his mistakes, practicing his left jab
FAVORITE TOY: His lucky blue PAW-XING gloves
MOTTO: "U gotta fight wiff ur brainz!"
LIFE DREAM: To open a PAW-XING gym with Brawn

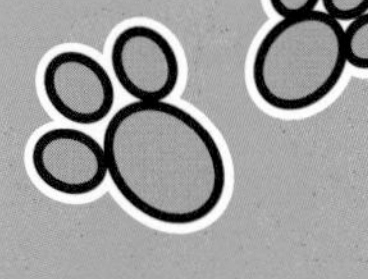

BRAWN

LIKES: Gains
DISLIKES: Carbs
FAVORITE SNACK: Muscle milk
HOBBIES: Pumping up at the gym, working on his right hook and UPPER-CAT
FAVORITE TOY: His shiny purple PAW-XING shorts
MOTTO: "Lickz like a kitten, bitez like a flea!"
LIFE DREAM: To tell the world about his FUR-RIENDSHIP with Brainz

MEET Liftz & Fliez!

Fliez always leaps before she looks. But that's okay, because Liftz is always there to stop her MEOWMENTUM right before she goes headfirst into the nearest wall! Liftz has always been there for Fliez and her crazy schemes—she's usually the one who makes sure they both make it out with all NINE OF THEIR LIVES. When Fliez wants to pretend to be a supercat and fling herself off of the roof? Liftz stacks MEOWTRESSES across the yard so her landing is as soft as goose feathers. Fliez just wants to feel the wind beneath her paws, and Liftz just wants Fliez to come home in one piece.

LIFTZ

LIKES: Standing with paws firmly planted on the ground
DISLIKES: Heights
FAVORITE SNACK: MICE KRISPIES treats
HOBBIES: Looking out for Fliez, catching Fliez, playing CAT-MINTON
FAVORITE TOY: Wind-up fish
MOTTO: "I iz here 2 lift u up."
LIFE DREAM: To make Fliez a pair of wings that work

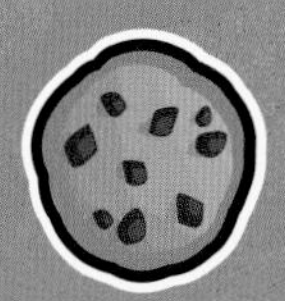

FLIEZ

LIKES: Heights
DISLIKES: Standing with paws firmly planted on the ground
FAVORITE SNACK: Airplane peanuts
HOBBIES: Doodling wings, jumping, leaping, climbing
FAVORITE TOY: Green MEOWDEL airplane
MOTTO: "Mah heart haz wingz!"
LIFE DREAM: To fly with her own wings and never come back down!

MEET Bongo & Bass!

Bongo and Bass are always kicking it island-style. Why worry about hairballs and bad fur days when you can put your paws up with a fresh cup of coconut milk? But despite the relaxing vibes of the island, Bongo has absolutely NO chill—his paws are always on the move, tippy-tapping a rhythm that only he can hear. **UN-FUR-TUNATELY** for Bass, Bongo has discovered that Bass's fur has the **PURR-FECT** tone for a jam. So when Bass settles down for a catnap on the beach, Bongo is there, tapping out a beat to make kitties move their feet!

BONGO

LIKES: Reggae MEOWSIC
DISLIKES: Sitting still
FAVORITE SNACK: Poi
HOBBIES: Hiking, drumming singing, swimming
FAVORITE TOY: Milk mug shaped like a Tiki head
MOTTO: "Grab life by the pawz!"
LIFE DREAM: To leave his island and share his songs with the world

BASS

LIKES: Sandcastles
DISLIKES: Feeling rushed
FAVORITE SNACK: Poke
HOBBIES: Relaxing, taking catnaps, hula dancing
FAVORITE TOY: Stuffed animal mouse with a grass skirt
MOTTO: "Iz time for catnap."
LIFE DREAM: To open up a surf shop near the beach

MEET Debbie & Downer

Downer is Debbie's reality check, and Debbie is Downer's...downfall. The two kitties have been friends since KIN-FUR-GARTEN, when Debbie launched herself at Downer in the middle of paw-print painting and splattered yellow paint all over his fur. Debbie is a leap-without-looking, "drink the milk without checking the expiration date" kind of kitty. Downer is a "prepare for the end of the world because it might end tomorrow," kind of kitty. Debbie and Downer might be as different as two kitties can be, but you'll never see Debbie without Downer by her side, and VICE FUR-SA.

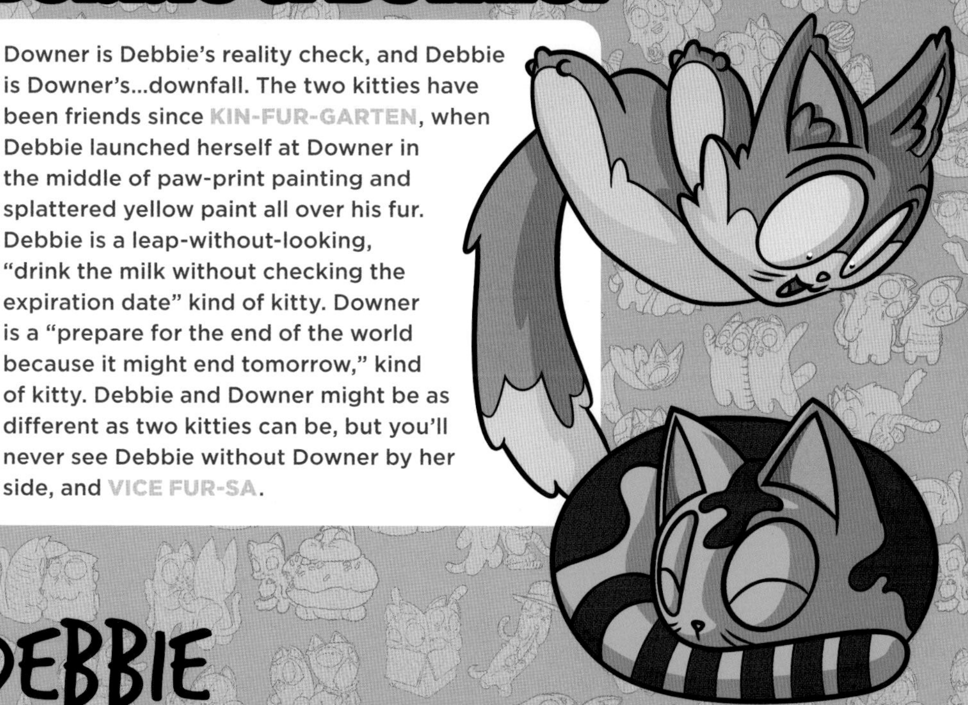

DEBBIE

LIKES: Surprise PAW-TIES, loud MEOWSIC, trying new things
DISLIKES: Staying home
FAVORITE SNACK: Jalapeño poppers
HOBBIES: Jumping on the trampoline, tackling Downer, chasing bugs
FAVORITE TOY: Mouse-shaped kite
MOTTO: "KITTEH INCOMING!"
LIFE DREAM: She really hasn't thought that far ahead...skydiving?

DOWNER

LIKES: Staying home
DISLIKES: Surprise PAW-TIES, loud MEOWSIC, trying new things
FAVORITE SNACK: Oatmeal
HOBBIES: Researching cat accident statistics, making tea, scrapbooking (with the extra-soft paper that doesn't give paper cuts)
FAVORITE TOY: Stuffed animal penguin
MOTTO: "I haz nothing 2 fear but—everything."
LIFE DREAM: To make it through all nine lives without CAT-ASTROPHIC injuries

MEET The Greatest & The Natest!

The Greatest and The Natest are training to be the most famous **ACRO-CATIC** duo around. They practice feats of strength and agility every day, hoping to flip, bounce, and soar their way to fame to the sound of wild **APPAWSE**! But The Greatest needs to hit the gym a little more. His paws can't lift anything bigger than a ball of yarn. And the Natest needs to cut down on his whipped cream and puffer fish parfaits, because he is *definitely* bigger than a ball of yarn. Show time!

THE GREATEST

LIKES: Challenging himself, signing PAW-TOGRAPHS
DISLIKES: Lifting weights
FAVORITE SNACK: Grapefruit
HOBBIES: Flexing in the mirror, practicing his winning smile
FAVORITE TOY: Yo-yo
MOTTO: "U can't upstage dah GREATEST"
LIFE DREAM: To go on tour with The Natest

THE NATEST

LIKES: Fame
DISLIKES: Not being able to fit into his ACRO-CAT costume

FAVORITE SNACK: Swordfish shish kabobs
HOBBIES: Thinking about using the treadmill, trying to reach toys without getting up
FAVORITE TOY: Treat ball with the broken latch
MOTTO: "Dah show must go on!"
LIFE DREAM: To hear the fans chant his name on stage

MEET Piggy & Bax!

Piggy and Bax were born in a hurry. Speedy sisters with the wind in their paws, these two are so in sync that when they run they sometimes look like one big kitty! Bax is the smaller of the two, but Piggy's always picking her up and racing away. This used to get them into trouble when they ran relay races—apparently you're supposed to run your leg of the race solo with no **KITTYBACK-RIDING** allowed. Oh, well. Giddyap!

PIGGY

LIKES: The wind in her whiskers, the blur in her fur
DISLIKES: Fences
FAVORITE SNACK: Fast food
HOBBIES: Racing, running, carrying Bax
FAVORITE TOY: Little yellow feather
MOTTO: "Gotz 2 go, FAST!"
LIFE DREAM: To teach Bax to carry her for once!

BAX

LIKES: Her tail trailing behind her, the weight of a baton in her paws
DISLIKES: Dead ends
FAVORITE SNACK: Takeout
HOBBIES: Darting, dashing, being lifted by Piggy
FAVORITE TOY: Purple sweatband
MOTTO: "Mah pawz don't PAUSE!"
LIFE DREAM: To carry Piggy across a finish line!

MEET Rightz & Leftz!

Rightz and Leftz are **NASCAT** superstars. Nothing gets them more excited than the sound of wheels screeching through skids. Lap after lap, mile after mile, these best friends have their eyes on the finish line! Okay, so maybe their racecars look more like their **FUR-VORITE** fuzzy slippers (one kitty per shoe) and maybe they haven't been to the **TAIL-A-DEGA MOTORWAY** (YET), but it's only a matter of time until they're getting handed more trophies than they can hold in their paws! Kitties, start your engines!

RIGHTZ

LIKES: Soft slippers on carpet
DISLIKES: Forgetting to tape a race
FAVORITE SNACK: Swedish fish
HOBBIES: Collecting PAW-TOGRAPHS of famous NASCAT racers , watching old races
FAVORITE TOY: The right-paw slipper (the best one)
MOTTO: "If ur not FIRST ur LAST!"
LIFE DREAM: To compete in (and finish) a NASCAT race

LEFTZ

LIKES: The roar of a NASCAT crowd cheering
DISLIKES: Falling over
FAVORITE SNACK: Sour gummy worms
HOBBIES: Posting NASCAT stats on KIT-STAGRAM, PAW-TICIPATING in a Fantasy NASCAT League
FAVORITE TOY: The left-paw slipper (the best one)
MOTTO: "Shake and bake, kittehs!"
LIFE DREAM: To cheer Rightz on in a NASCAT race (and maybe just ride PAW-SSENGER for now)

MEET Sir Singz & Sheila Songz!

5, 6, 7, 8! Sir Singz and Sheila Songz are ready for their big break, and they won't take "no" for an answer. Okay, they *have* taken "no" for an answer...about fifty times. But their "yes" is right around the corner! Sir Singz is descended from a circus tiger who could burp poetry. Sheila Songz's family invented the game **PRANCE, PRANCE, REVOLUTION**. This power couple has the moves, the grooves, and the shiny white smiles of show biz down to a science. Now they have to show the judges that **THESE TAILS CAN'T FAIL**!

SIR SINGZ

LIKES: Show tunes, MEOWSICAL FLEA-TER
DISLIKES: Posers (this industry isn't just for ANYKITTY)
FAVORITE SNACK: The tears of his competitors
HOBBIES: TAP-PRANCING, JAZZ PAWS, sending catnip baskets to PAW-DUCERS
FAVORITE TOY: His lucky microphone
MOTTO: "Talent iz all about cattitude!"
LIFE DREAM: To star in a FUR-OADWAY show

SHEILA SONGZ

LIKES: Swing PRANCING, the tango
DISLIKES: Rejection (don't they know who she *is*?)
FAVORITE SNACK: The taste of the spotlight
HOBBIES: Doing vocal warm-ups, CLAWSTUME designing, stretching
FAVORITE TOY: Her FUR-VORITE leotard
MOTTO: "Practice makez purr-fect!"
LIFE DREAM: To be the lead in a MEOWSICAL

MEET Leany & Tippy!

Leany and Tippy are...weird. Their eyes seem to follow you from room to room, even if their paws don't move. And no kitty has seen them blink...ever. Leany and Tippy don't talk much, but they're as thick as **FLEAS**. They do everything together, from staring at other kitties in the kitchen while they're taking their milk break, to staring at other kitties out the window when it's sunny outside, to staring at other kitties in the dead of night when they're fast asleep...

LEANY

LIKES: Ghost stories (stories told by ghosts)
DISLIKES: Sunny spots
FAVORITE SNACK: Catnip calzone
HOBBIES: Staring, peering, peeking
FAVORITE TOY: Fish bone
MOTTO: "Oh sorry. Waz I staring?"
LIFE DREAM: To win a staring contest with Tippy

TIPPY

LIKES: Spying
DISLIKES: Attention
FAVORITE SNACK: Fruit gummies
HOBBIES: Gawking, stalking, appearing silently in rooms
FAVORITE TOY: Black watch
MOTTO: "I iz keepin' an eye out. Alwayz."
LIFE DREAM: To win a staring contest with Leany

#PURRFECTPAIR

MEET
Carl & Judy!

Carl has always been **SMITTEN AS A KITTEN** with Judy. But Carl is the clumsiest kitty ever. **PURR-OM NIGHT** ended in disaster when he caused the photobooth to collapse! But Judy loves Carl the most when he's tipping and slipping. When she first fell for him, he was falling. He had slipped on a muffin on the floor of the **CAT-FETERIA** and fell into the macaroni salad. Judy thought macaroni had never looked so handsome. **ME-OWW**!

CARL

LIKES: Judy
DISLIKES: Falling on his tail
FAVORITE SNACK: Rocky Road MICE CREAM
HOBBIES: Blushing, staring at Judy, doing the accidental kitty-splits
FAVORITE TOY: His beautiful blue bowtie
MOTTO: "It takes skillz to trip over nothing!"
LIFE DREAM: To PAW-POSE to Judy

JUDY

LIKES: Carl
DISLIKES: Having to take Carl to the PAW-SPITAL
FAVORITE SNACK: MEOWCARONI salad
HOBBIES: Making Carl blush, taking pictures, looking out for slippery spots
FAVORITE TOY: Silver fur brush
MOTTO: "My pawz may be solid, but I fallz for u."
LIFE DREAM: To marry Carl

MEET Purr & Plexed!

Purr and Plexed have a lot of questions. First of all, why were kitties put on the planet? And why oh why does milk taste so good? Purr and Plexed are here to find answers. They meet every day to work on their book: *Kitties Explained: A Feline Guide for When Ur Feelin' Confused*. But the questions don't stop when the kitties are ready to write, and all they have finished so far is the title page! Some kitties say they'll never finish their book because all they do is ask questions. But Purr and Plexed are just worried that curiosity will kill the cats!

PURR

LIKES: Unsolved mysteries
DISLIKES: Unsolved mysteries
FAVORITE SNACK: Hot dogs (but, are they made out of dogs?)
HOBBIES: Questioning, looking curious, reading CAT-SPIRACY blogs
FAVORITE TOY: The chewed up yellow game piece from an old game of Clue
MOTTO: "Wait. What?"
LIFE DREAM: To go on a book-signing tour. Wait, no—to finish his book.

PLEXED

LIKES: Calling help lines
DISLIKES: Books without glossaries
FAVORITE SNACK: Hot Pockets (but, are they made out of pockets?)
HOBBIES: Querying, appearing smart when he's actually confused
FAVORITE TOY: A pair of glasses with the lenses popped out
MOTTO: "I iz having a brain freeze."
LIFE DREAM: To try and stay grounded after his inevitable success makes his brain even bigger

#PURRFECTPAIR

MEET Sitz & Fitz!

For Sitz, sitting is an art form, a quest, a calling. Sitz is Fitz's trainer, her right-hand kitty, and he knows just where to sit to keep her on her paws (or, well, off of them). Flexible Fitz is a **PAW-FESSIONAL CAT-TORTIONIST**, and in her off-season she trains with Sitz to stay limber. Nooks and crannies are no match for the seemingly liquid Fitz, and Sitz keeps her in tip-top shape. Or, top-tip shape—it really depends on what container she's in. How can Fitz fit without Sitz?

SITZ

LIKES: MEOWMORY foam

DISLIKES: Spiky surfaces

FAVORITE SNACK: MEWBERRY pie

HOBBIES: Perching, taking a seat, popping a squat

FAVORITE TOY: His paw-shaped stopwatch

MOTTO: "Never quitz when u can sitz!"

LIFE DREAM: To start a CAT-SULTATION business sitting for other CAT-TORTIONISTS

FITZ

LIKES: Going boneless

DISLIKES: Coughing up hairballs when she's in a tight space

FAVORITE SNACK: Tootsie rolls

HOBBIES: Wedging, shoving, squeezing

FAVORITE TOY: Pink wand toy

MOTTO: "Why stand out when u were made to fitz in?"

LIFE DREAM: To be the most famous CAT-TORTIONIST in HISS-TORY

Meet Frank & Tammy!

Frank and Tammy are lost. Well, that's what Frank thinks. He knows that Tammy should have taken that left he recommended, four or five streets back. But Tammy is **PAW-SITIVE** that Frank's hat must be a little too tight around his ears, because she did go left! These kitties have gotten lost more times than they can count! But nothing is going to make them miss this vacation. Now, is the GPS really telling them that this swamp is a shortcut?

FRANK

LIKES: Maps (he is the one who can read them, after all)
DISLIKES: When the map changes ("I'm telling you, they changed it! I know where I'm going!")
FAVORITE SNACK: Sunflower seeds
HOBBIES: Fishing, dozing, stocking up on sunscreen
FAVORITE TOY: His stylish blue hat
MOTTO: "Iz all right here in dah map!"
LIFE DREAM: To visit each of the Seven Wonders of the World

TAMMY

LIKES: Traveling
DISLIKES: When Frank mixes up north and south
FAVORITE SNACK: Trail mix
HOBBIES: Getting fur massages, collecting souvenirs in her FUR-NY pack
FAVORITE TOY: Her trusty fur-ny pack—do you need any gum?
MOTTO: "That'z upside-down, Frank."
LIFE DREAM: To spend a whole week on the beach with her toe beans in the sand

#PURRFECTPAIR

MEET Wabbitz & DaHat!

DaHat is an aspiring **MEOWGICIAN**, but his brother Wabbitz is an aspiring prankster. The problem is, Wabbitz is really forgetful. So when he went to switch DaHat's magic wand with a licorice stick, he ended up getting distracted and eating the magic wand before he'd even made the swap. And when he tried to tie DaHat's magic rope into knots, he lost track of the cord and ended up tying his tail instead! So if you see the Great and **PAW-ERFUL** DaHat's **MEOWGIC** show, and Wabbitz pops out of his hat instead of a bunny...chances are it's another prank gone wrong!

WABBITZ

LIKES: Pulling pranks
DISLIKES: Getting caught in DaHat's MEOWGIC box
FAVORITE SNACK: Soft pretzels
HOBBIES: Pranking DaHat, snoozing on a deck of DaHat's MEOWGIC cards
FAVORITE TOY: Glittery green ball of yarn
MOTTO: "Presto, cat-o!"
LIFE DREAM: To have his own prankster TV show

DAHAT

LIKES: The shocked gasps of a crowd after he does a trick
DISLIKES: When Wabbitz accidentally releases all of his trick doves
FAVORITE SNACK: Skittles
HOBBIES: Practicing new tricks, hiding props from Wabbitz
FAVORITE TOY: His magic wand
MOTTO: "Ala-cat-zam!"
LIFE DREAM: To get a lovely assistant

PURRFECTPAIR

MEET
Mary & Larry!

Mary and Larry are **A-MEOWICA'S** Sweethearts, starring in over twenty romantic dramas and **PAW-MEDIES**. Their first movie took place on a cruise ship, and the chemistry was downright **PAW-PABLE.** Movie posters of the two actors sell almost as well as the movies themselves! Onscreen, it may look like kitty love, but off-screen, Mary and Larry are just **FUR-RIENDS**. Both actors have moved on to other projects, but they never want to let go of their first movie together. So, they take a trip to the ocean every year just to relive the **MEOWGIC**! **PURR-FECT**!

MARY

LIKES: CELINE FLEA-ON, CLAWMUNITY theater
DISLIKES: Doing her own stunts
FAVORITE SNACK: PAW-VOCADO toast
HOBBIES: Attending PAW-MIERES, drinking sparkling milk at charity galas
FAVORITE TOY: Her A-CAT-EMY Award
MOTTO: "I iz a star!"
LIFE DREAM: To quit acting and start directing

LARRY

LIKES: HISS-TORICAL fiction, MEOWTHED acting
DISLIKES: When kitties talk in the movie theater
FAVORITE SNACK: Kombucha
HOBBIES: Rehearsing scripts, learning cues, giving interviews
FAVORITE TOY: Old film camera
MOTTO: "Iz ready for my close-up!"
LIFE DREAM: To break out of romance and into CAT-VENTURE roles

TABLE4TWO

MEET Cooks & Toppinz!

Cooks is inspired by food; tickled by tuna, smitten with salmon, and over-the-top taken in by trout. He ignores the recipe and measures ingredients by what's in his heart. And his heart, like his stomach, always says: more, more, more! Toppinz loves the way Cooks dances around the oven, tossing spices like they're confetti and always taste-testing his FUR-VORITE meals. He's an artist in the kitchen, she just wishes that his canvas didn't include her coat—do you know how hard it is to get pepperoni out of fur?

COOKS

LIKES: Licking salt from his paws, smelling a simmering pot
DISLIKES: Slicing onions—chefs should only cry from joy!
FAVORITE SNACK: FUR-LET mignon with a side of braised catnip
HOBBIES: Stirring, sizzling, creating culinary MEOWSTERPIECES
FAVORITE TOY: His chef's hat
MOTTO: "Dah secret ingredient iz MILKZ."
LIFE DREAM: To open his own restaurant: The Catnip Café

TOPPINZ

LIKES: Snuggling up against a boiling pot of water
DISLIKES: Smoke alarms
FAVORITE SNACK: Clam chowder
HOBBIES: Falling asleep in the crisper drawer, trying to get the garlic smell out of her whiskers
FAVORITE TOY: Green spinning top
MOTTO: "Oh, am I snoozin in ur soup?"
LIFE DREAM: To have a special cat bed built into the side of the stove

MEET Goldz & Fishez!

Goldz and Fishez aren't exactly great at catching fish—their catlike reflexes need a lot of work. They'd prefer their fish to come to them in an easily opened can, already cut into bite-sized pieces, but they are determined to prove that they can reel in the meals with the best of them! So far, all they've had are empty bowls. In fact, their last fishy "meal" got so far down the road that he got adopted by the local aquarium and has his own exhibit. **ARE YOU KITTEN ME?**

GOLDZ

LIKES: Seeing how many anchovies he can fit in his mouth
DISLIKES: Losing his bait to sneaky fish
FAVORITE SNACK: Fish sticks
HOBBIES: Munching, crunching, sleeping off a big meal
FAVORITE TOY: Stuffed animal trout
MOTTO: "Somethin' smellz fishy."
LIFE DREAM: To catch the biggest fish the world has ever seen!

FISHEZ

LIKES: Super-spicy fish sauce
DISLIKES: Getting the seafood sweats
FAVORITE SNACK: Jellyfish tentacles
HOBBIES: Hitting up shrimp buffets, challenging Goldz to eating contests
FAVORITE TOY: Squeaky rubber whale for bathtime
MOTTO: "I can haz fishy?"
LIFE DREAM: To catch and cook at LEAST one fish. Just one!

MEET Yawn & Drooler!

Yawn and Drooler are going to do big things. Yawn is going to discover a cure for **TAIL-ACHES**! Drooler is going to create a brand-new, hairball-resistant fabric! Just as soon as they finish this catnap. See, Yawn and Drooler are just two snores away from being the best of the best! Just one drool droplet away from taking the world by storm! Just a few tail-twitching dreams from total **PAW-MINATION**. But **RIGHT MEOW** they're the best at snoozing, and you don't want to quit a race while you're ahead...

YAWN

LIKES: Electric blankets
DISLIKES: Falling off the cat bed
FAVORITE SNACK: Pumpkin pie
HOBBIES: Dreaming, dozing, resting
FAVORITE TOY: Special star-shaped pillow
MOTTO: "I can sleep wiff mah eyez closed."
LIFE DREAM: To go down in HISS-TORY as the most impressive kitty ever

DROOLER

LIKES: Feather pillows
DISLIKES: Sleepwalking
FAVORITE SNACK: Potato soup
HOBBIES: Snoring, yawning, slumbering
FAVORITE TOY: Purple fleece kitten blanket
MOTTO: "I alwayz haz good dreamz!"
LIFE DREAM: To be elected as PURR-ESIDENT

TABLE4TWO

MEET

Sir Spoon & Mr. Sammy!

Sir Spoon and Mr. Sammy are two **BIG CITY CATS** who've decided to take to the country for some peace and quiet. But as it turns out—they hate both peace AND quiet! Sir Spoon can't sleep without the racket of traffic, and Mr. Sammy is allergic to hay. The WiFi stopped working a few days ago, and these two friends would kill for a latte, so now they just have to figure out how to bring all this farm-fresh cow's milk back to the city...**YUM!**

SIR SPOON

LIKES: The subway
DISLIKES: Forks
FAVORITE SNACK: Salmon soup
HOBBIES: Using public transportation, trying out new restaurants (spoon in paw!)
FAVORITE TOY: His silver spoon
MOTTO: "I iz the city and the city iz me."
LIFE DREAM: To afford a loft with no roommate

MR. SAMMY

LIKES: Street food carts
DISLIKES: Nature
FAVORITE SNACK: FUR-OSTED mini-wheats
HOBBIES: Going to gallery openings, gazing at skyscrapers
FAVORITE TOY: Flashing yellow laser light
MOTTO: "Hey! I iz walkin' here!"
LIFE DREAM: To graffiti his name on a building in MEW YORK

#TABLE4TWO

MEET Doughy & Nutz!

Doughy and Nutz opened their bakery years ago and they still haven't made a **PURR-OFIT**! The two friends just don't get it. Sure, they might nab a treat or two from their inventory...but if anyone can take a little **SKIM MILK** off the top, they can! Okay, so there was that one morning Doughy ate all of the catnip cookies. But in his defense, they are SUPER delicious! Nutz has been handling the kitty cash—he's the one that got a degree from that online college that isn't open anymore...why they aren't rolling in the dough is a total **MEOWSTERY**!

DOUGHY

LIKES: Sugar, syrup, salt, carbs

DISLIKES: An empty stomach

FAVORITE SNACK: The one that started it all...donuts!

HOBBIES: Giving in to cravings, watching the Food Network

FAVORITE TOY: Saltshaker filled with sprinkles

MOTTO: "Iz alwayz time for cake!"

LIFE DREAM: To have a MICE CREAM flavor named after him

NUTZ

LIKES: Cashews, almonds, peanuts, macadamias

DISLIKES: Questions about his college degree

FAVORITE SNACK: Nutella

HOBBIES: Forgetting to lock the bakery, taking catnaps behind the counter

FAVORITE TOY: Spatula with the cracked handle

MOTTO: "U haz 2 spend milk money 2 make milk money!"

LIFE DREAM: To start turning a PURR-OFIT

MEET Terri & Yaki

Terri and Yaki are sisters who love sushi so much that they have dreams about miso soup. Yaki even works at a sushi restaurant where her employee discount gets her all the raw fish she can handle. But Terri has the memory of a goldfish, and Yaki's work UNI-FURM makes her look like a giant sushi roll. Yaki's been bitten by a confused Terri so many times, she's started naming her bruises after her sister. But that's just how they ROLL!

TERRI

LIKES: Fish!
DISLIKES: ...not getting to have fish!
FAVORITE SNACK: Ooh, fish!
HOBBIES: Trying to remember, doing brain teasers, playing with Yaki
FAVORITE TOY: Orange feather wand...she thinks
MOTTO: "Oopz. I forgot!"
LIFE DREAM: To remember everything without any effort!

YAKI

LIKES: Soy sauce
DISLIKES: Tail bites
FAVORITE SNACK: Salmon sashimi
HOBBIES: Waitressing, leaving notes for Terri so she'll remember things
FAVORITE TOY: Catnip koi fish
MOTTO: "Sushi givez me the feelz."
LIFE DREAM: To get Terri a job at the restaurant

MEET Shorty & Smallz!

Smallz is just a little bit worried **RIGHT MEOW**. Okay, a lot of the time. Okay—all of the time. But don't you know what's out there? There are big dogs with giant teeth, ghosts haunting underneath cat beds, and don't even get her started on *water*! I mean, who thought *baths* were a good idea? Shorty is only worried about one thing: Smallz. Sure, Smallz is a **SCAREDY-CAT**, but that's why her best **FUR-RIEND** Shorty is a brave one! If something scary wants to get to Smallz, it'll have to get through Shorty first!

SHORTY

LIKES: Horror MEW-VIES
DISLIKES: Seeing SMALLZ A-FURAID
FAVORITE SNACK: Barbeque potato chips
HOBBIES: Keeping a sharp eye out for danger, distracting Smallz with head boops
FAVORITE TOY: Wool sock puppet
MOTTO: "I iz no scaredy-cat!"
LIFE DREAM: To cure Smallz of her fear of baths (she really needs one)

SMALLZ

LIKES: Pillow forts
DISLIKES: YOWL-A-WEEN, dogs, ghosts, water, scary-looking squirrels, fast-flying bugs
FAVORITE SNACK: Grilled cheese sandwiches with tomato soup
HOBBIES: Hiding, peeking out of well-lit areas, putting paws over her eyes
FAVORITE TOY: Her stuffed animal kitty, Anthony
MOTTO: "AAAAH! SAVE URSELF!"
LIFE DREAM: To face one of her fears (or at least stop adding to the list)

TWOCUTE

MEET Smoosh & Moosh!

Smoosh likes to be close. No, closer than that. Nope, eeeven closer...**PURR-FECT**! Smoosh needs to be right in your whiskers, right there in the action! Moosh acts annoyed when Smoosh gets all up in his kitty business, but he secretly loves to cuddle. But even though Smoosh is a **SWEETIE PAW**, when she falls asleep, her back legs start bunny-kicking and her claws start swiping like they have a mind of their own. Sleepy Smoosh is a whole other kitty, and Moosh spends his naps dodging her swats and snores.

SMOOSH

LIKES: Cuddles
DISLIKES: PAW-SONAL space
FAVORITE SNACK: Fudge
HOBBIES: Snuggling, nuzzling, staring at Moosh when she thinks he's not looking
FAVORITE TOY: Orange rattle ball
MOTTO: "Iz no such thing as purr-sonal space."
LIFE DREAM: To have Moosh be the one to start a cuddle puddle

MOOSH

LIKES: Sweater weather
DISLIKES: When Smoosh kicks him off the cat bed in her sleep
FAVORITE SNACK: FIG MEWTONS
HOBBIES: Nudging Smoosh, taking three-hour catnaps, watching the DISCOV-FURRY Channel
FAVORITE TOY: Green cat bed with the lumpy corners
MOTTO: "Why burr when u can purr?"
LIFE DREAM: To buy a bigger cat bed to avoid Sleepy Smoosh injuries

MEET Lovey & Dovey!

Lovey and Dovey are as close as two kitties can be. When Lovey takes a step, Dovey takes a step. When Lovey chases the laser light, Dovey chases the laser light. When Lovey coughs up a hairball, Dovey eats that hairball. They complete each other! No kitty is sure how Lovey and Dovey can stand so much time together, but one thing is FUR SURE: these two are meant to be together FUR-EVER, no matter what!

LOVEY

LIKES:	Dovey
DISLIKES:	Summer camp
FAVORITE SNACK:	Twizzlers
HOBBIES:	Brushing her fur just like Dovey's, snoozing in twin cat beds
FAVORITE TOY:	Double-headed scratching post
MOTTO:	"2 kitties iz twice as nice!"
LIFE DREAM:	To have a reality show with Dovey

DOVEY

LIKES:	Lovey
DISLIKES:	Solo bathroom breaks
FAVORITE SNACK:	Red Vines
HOBBIES:	Hugging Lovey, trading places with Lovey to fake out other kitties
FAVORITE TOY:	Side-by-side cat dancers
MOTTO:	"Double the snugz, none of the strugz!"
LIFE DREAM:	Whatever Lovey wants to do!

MEET Mitts & Gloves!

Mitts and Gloves were hired as co-hosts of a kitten's show called "Are You Pulling My Tail?" where they teach kittens manners. Their episode about washing your paws after your morning milkshake was so **PAW-PULAR** that it went viral on **MEWTUBE**! From that point on, Mitts and Gloves have been huge stars, and they can't even **CATWALK** down the street anymore without being recognized by an excited kitten (or three). But fame didn't change these two peppy kitties: they're always happy to stop and do their signature **PAW-SHAKE** for fans!

MITTS

LIKES: Group PAW-JECTS, Ping-Pong tournaments
DISLIKES: Losing touch with old FUR-RIENDS
FAVORITE SNACK: Funyuns
HOBBIES: Meeting fans, filming episodes, playing touch football
FAVORITE TOY: Little rubber football with the chewed-up laces
MOTTO: "I iz ALWAYZ excited!"
LIFE DREAM: To do a spinoff show for teen kitties

GLOVES

LIKES: Slapping paws with other kitties—high-five!
DISLIKES: Waking up early on CATURDAYS
FAVORITE SNACK: Sun Chips
HOBBIES: Going over scripts, visiting sick fans in the PAW-SPITAL
FAVORITE TOY: Red lanyard
MOTTO: "Let'z do dis!"
LIFE DREAM: To start a charity for kittens

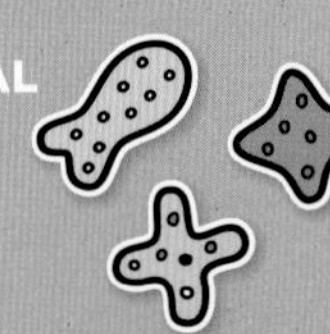

MEET Topperz & Mr. Miffed!

Mr. Miffed used to be a lone kitty. A solo act. A renegade cat with nothing to tie him down. That is, until Topperz came along. Topperz was a kitten born a block away. She trotted in one day like she owned the place, stood on his head, and fell fast asleep. No kitty is brave enough to do that to Mr. Miffed! But there's something about Topperz that makes her IM-PAWSSIBLE to say "no" to. Before Mr. Miffed knew it, she was stealing his blanket and taking up PURR-MANENT residence on her favorite cat bed: his head.

TOPPERZ

LIKES: Fur under her paws
DISLIKES: Sleeping outside
FAVORITE SNACK: PAW-MESAN cheese
HOBBIES: Tugging on Mr. Miffed's tail, snoozing on Mr. Miffed's head, stealing Mr. Miffed's milk
FAVORITE TOY: Ball with the bell inside
MOTTO: "What'z urs iz mine!"
LIFE DREAM: To get Mr. Miffed to adopt another kitten just like her

LIKES: PURR-IVACY
DISLIKES: Lack of PURR-SONAL space
FAVORITE SNACK: Chicken noodle soup
HOBBIES: Ignoring Topperz, PAW-TENDING not to care when Topperz catnaps on his head
FAVORITE TOY: Pink scratching post
MOTTO: "Kittenz iz dangerous!"
LIFE DREAM: To get rid of the FUR-EELOADER, Topperz...at some point...maybe

MEET Squeezy & Squishy!

Squeezy and Squishy never met a box they didn't like. And they've never met a box they couldn't fit *into*. Cereal box? They've napped in that. Poster tubes? Done and done. Mailbox? Duh. What are they, amateurs? No kitty is more liquid than these two brothers, and they never scrunch into a box alone. **IF THEY BOTH DON'T FIT, THEY BOTH DON'T SIT**—that's the golden rule. Don't mess with a kitty's right to squish. Ever.

SQUEEZY

LIKES: The comforting hug of cardboard
DISLIKES: Ring boxes (what is the point of those? You couldn't fit a whisker in those!)
FAVORITE SNACK: Tissue paper
HOBBIES: Cramming, crunching, squeezing
FAVORITE TOY: An old kibble box that still smells fresh
MOTTO: "U gotta fit it 2 win it!"
LIFE DREAM: To make a tunnel system of boxes from the kitchen to the mail slot

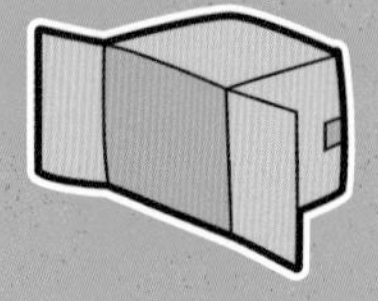

SQUISHY

LIKES: The smell of packing peanuts
DISLIKES: Accidentally flattening a box
FAVORITE SNACK: Packing tape
HOBBIES: Scrunching, crushing, squishing
FAVORITE TOY: An old refrigerator box (it's like a mansion in there!)
MOTTO: "Iz no such thing as an empty box!"
LIFE DREAM: To sign up for a subscription box of empty boxes—delivered daily

I CAN
HAZ
FISHY?
IZ NUFFIN
TO SEE
HERE

I'M MAKIN' MY MEOWSTERPIECE!

WE SING WIFF OUR HEARTS!

GIMME FOODS

I HAZ PAWS
OF FURY

LOOK OUT BELOW!

IZ TIME TO VROOM!

NOW!